M000304096

BROOMSTICKS AND BOARD GAMES

A Spooky Games Club Mystery Book 1

AMY MCNULTY

Crimson Fox
PUBLISHING

Broomsticks and Board Games by Amy McNulty

© 2020 by Amy McNulty. All rights reserved.

No part of this book may be reproduced or transmitted in any form, including written, electronic, recording, or photocopying, without written permission of the author. The exception would be in the case of brief quotations embodied in critical articles or reviews.

Published by Crimson Fox Publishing, PO Box 1035, Turner, OR 97392

Cover design by Amy McNulty and RebecaCovers.

The characters and events appearing in this work are fictitious. Existing brands and businesses are used in a fictitious manner, and the author claims no ownership of or affiliation with trademarked properties. Any resemblance to real persons, living or dead, is purely coincidental, and not intended by the author.

ISBN: 978-1-952667-17-6

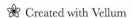 Created with Vellum

Chapter One

"*W*ow. That's a striking tattoo."

When you're doing your neighbor a favor by rummaging through his attic and someone walks up behind you while you're levitating just a *little* bit, you have three options.

One: Play it cool and float back down to the top of the stepstool, hoping he doesn't notice the smooth move.

Two: Admit the jig is up and introduce some poor hapless individual to the fact that witches—and vampires and werewolves and just about anything paranormal you can think of—are real.

Three: Lose your wits and tumble helplessly backward, right into the stranger's arms.

I, of course, stumbled into option three.

"Whoa, watch it!"

The deep, baritone voice was paired with a set of muscular arms in a white collared dress shirt. My back slammed against a sturdy chest, the top of my head clipping what had to be a chiseled chin—the grunt of pain that followed confirming my fears.

And then somehow, I found myself in a princess carry, my wavy, red-orange hair tumbling over the side of those muscular arms. Something hard pushed into my back as I gazed up into the dark brown eyes of a hopelessly handsome, completely unknown face.

This was Luna Lane. There weren't supposed to be unknown faces.

"Hi, there." He arched a single dark brow, the corner of his lips curling up into a smile, revealing a dazzling set of teeth.

The smallest trickle of blood cracked across his lips, dripping onto the perfectly centered cleft on his strong chin.

"Oh, bananaberries! I'm so sorry." My heart thumped rapidly—whether from the fact that I was in a tall, strapping stranger's arms or the fact that I'd clearly injured him or the *not so minor detail* that I really had no idea how much he'd seen.

Kicking and flailing, I scrambled to get back on my own two black-ballet-slippered feet. The groan the stranger let out when my elbow knocked into his wire-framed circular glasses didn't help matters.

I was two for two in the unintentionally-assaulting-a-stranger department today.

Good thing Sheriff Roan Birch had known me since I'd been just an apple in my mom's eye.

"Are you all right?" the man asked, one hand clutching a silver metal flashlight that he hadn't turned on yet. The other hand he used to straighten his glasses and wipe his chin. The bleeding had stopped already.

I stared up at him. At five-nine, I was still just barely up to this behemoth's shoulders. Huh. Not too often were there men that much taller than me in the Luna Lane dating pool.

Not that I was *at all* worried about dating this man whom I didn't know from Adam, of course.

Like a fish gasping for water, I clumsily opened my mouth. "I hope *you're* fine. I didn't mean to hurt you when I... When I..."

"Fell off the stepstool?" He took in the rickety, chipped stool sorely in need of a coat of paint— fixing that would surely count as a "good deed," actually, I needed to make a note of that—and let out a giant sigh.

He hadn't noticed.

My left arm itched something fierce, a sharp jolt of pain piercing into my very flesh. I scratched at the little patch of skin about the size of a quarter that was the source of the distress.

The rosy pink skin was changing, a scale the color of silver to match the rest of the scales that coiled up and down my arm, from shoulder to wrist, branching out in all directions like a growing vine.

My shiny, silver "tattoo" that wasn't a *tattoo* at all.

"Bananaberries," I swore. "What time is it?"

He tilted his chin. "I think it's around seven…"

Sunset was at 6:54 today. It had to be too late.

I was getting *way* too laid back about this. I'd *sworn* I'd had time. It'd just take a minute to help Milton Woodward out next door, get my good deed out of the way for the day—right *at the end of* the day.

Hubris, thy name is Dahlia Poplar.

"What are you doing?" asked the stranger, loosening the simple red tie around his neck and sliding in behind me as I climbed the stepstool once more.

I slipped on the third stair. This thing really *was* in need of repair. My eyes flit to the sole window in Milton's attic, the last embers of the orange sky over the horizon.

No time to repair a stepstool, especially without magic. *Focus, Dahlia. Stick to what you're in here for.*

"Careful," said the man, sliding in to offer support.

Support I wouldn't have needed at all if the guy would just *leave me alone* already.

Balancing on the very top, I stretched my left arm out again, wincing as the scale burned into my flesh.

No. It's not too late. It's not!

I pulled my arm back and reached out with my right. *Almost there.*

My fingers grazed the long, rectangular box Milton had asked me to get down for him.

It was yellowing and faded, the beams from that small attic window reaching perfectly onto the box for years and years, no doubt, the edges of the top of the box frayed from frequent, perhaps careless, removal.

Almost had it. Almost, but not quite close enough. This was why I'd been using a levitating enchantment to begin with.

Why in the blazes had Milton stored it up so far out of reach to begin with?

With a scream, I fell back, the small patch on my left arm too painful to ignore any longer, the new silver stone scale ripping into the flesh permanently.

The man behind me wrapped his arms around me, the flashlight still clutched in his hand, and we both tumbled down the last couple of steps on the stool.

The yowl I let out led him to quickly steady me and look down at my feet.

"Did you twist your ankle?" he asked.

My arm smarted enough that my first instinct was to snap at him—to blame him for my failure, for my ego thinking I could quickly get a good deed done and out of the way with only a few minutes to spare. But as I cradled the new scale on my left arm and looked at the man in the dying light, I bit my tongue.

"I'm fine," I muttered, just a little bit of the sullenness I felt permeating my voice. "Thank you,"

I added quickly, staring at the hardwood floor. There were knots in the wood that reminded me of ghostly faces staring up at me to mock Luna Lane's last remaining witch for her foolishness.

With a click, the man turned on his flashlight, illuminating the dark space with a dim, yellow beam. My eyes strained to adjust as he climbed up the rickety stepstool and took the box down off the top shelf with no trouble whatsoever, climbing back and handing the dusty board game box labeled "Evidence" to me with both hands as if a present.

Evidence, huh? Is that a Clue rip-off?

Curse his long limbs, the short stepstool—me having to hide the fact that I could have levitated and gotten it myself.

Curse foolish me for not acting sooner.

"Thanks," I said quietly, taking the game. I couldn't look at him.

I could have used levitation to bring the box right down to me the moment I'd entered the room. But good deeds didn't work that way on a very technical level.

Good deeds. I'd been cursed—before I'd been born, mind you—to have to perform one every single day of my life before the sun fully set or I'd slowly—one scale at a time—turn to stone.

That was what the shiny, silver "tattoo" was. A record of my failure.

And the older I got, the bigger each new scale seemed to be.

Examining my arm, I could see that I'd clearly had a lot of days that had been failures. But I couldn't have rightly fully performed a good deed per day as an infant and young child. Mom had tried her best, cajoling me into picking up litter or setting the table at a friend's house before dinner, but the *intent* had to be there.

The understanding.

It had only been with Mom's magic that we'd been able to keep the scales so tiny to begin with. It was the most she'd been able to do for me, to save me from the dark magic that ran through my veins.

I was certain the witch who'd cursed me had assumed I'd be fully stone before I'd reached my third birthday.

But no. I'd survived far longer than that. I was thirty now and still here, my stone-scaled arm the only evidence I'd ever been doomed to die young.

The last ten years, with Mom gone, there was nothing I could do to keep the scales small anymore.

So it was a good thing I was pretty vigilant about doing good deeds to help everyone out. Mostly vigilant. Okay, I was a little lax about it, but…

Luna Lane was a small town. Good deeds hardly ever encompassed saving lives or making sure someone didn't go hungry for the night.

There were three hundred of us. In general, the town was full of people who took care of one another.

There were almost no good deeds left to go around to stretch three hundred and sixty-five days a year.

And I couldn't step foot outside of this town to help anyone elsewhere.

That dug extra deep. I knew there was so much good my powers could do outside of our tiny town, but the curse... The curse hadn't been some way to encourage benevolence.

It had been a mockery. A twisted mockery of the kind of witch my mom had become, always helping others, never using her magic to curse people, to cause even the mildest form of mischief.

I took a deep breath. I shouldn't have been so quick to "curse" anything, not even jokingly in my head, least of all this amiable stranger.

I stared at the box. It was a game from the 1960s or 70s by the looks of it. Milton and his wife, Leana, had played games a lot when I'd been growing up, but this one was completely unfamiliar.

This was the first time he'd asked for a game since his wife had passed earlier this year. He usually didn't remember she'd passed at all. He was always asking for her.

If only I could use healing magic on him and heal the mixed-up memories in his brain.

"Some good deeds are just out of our hands," Mom would say. She hadn't been here when Milton had started exhibiting signs of dementia, but she'd tried to heal old Mrs. Flores when I'd been young.

Her mind hadn't wanted to accept the magic, Mom had decided. *"Just let her keep offering you blue-berry pie,"* she'd said when Mrs. Flores had confused a loaf of bread for the pie and had handed me the whole loaf on a plate. *"Smile. Thank her for it. She used to win ribbons for her pie, you know."*

Mrs. Flores was gone now, but the effect was the same. They were happier reminiscing in the less painful past.

So I wouldn't mess with Milton's brain. I'd just do one good deed at a time to help.

For a good deed to count, I couldn't fully rely on magic to accomplish the task. Again, it was a twisted mockery of my mom's intentions. If she played with the humans, she should help them like one.

In this case, Milton had wished he could play this game I'd never heard of again. To accomplish that, I'd had to figure out where it was—he'd kept saying, "the attic, the attic, she stuffed it away in the attic," and that was all I'd had to go on, so it'd taken longer than I'd hoped. I'd searched the place up and down, sweat sticking to my skin as the stuffiness of the musty attic had crushed down on me. If it hadn't been for an errant mouse scurrying up over the shelves and overhead beams, I never would have found it. Honestly, the Woodwards would have had to have gone out of their way to stuff that game so high up. No wonder he'd lost track of it.

Then, when I'd spotted the stepstool in the corner, I'd known I'd have to climb it like a human would have. Then—and only then—if I exhausted all possible options, could I cheat the system just a little bit. Levitate *myself*, not the object of my desire. Besides, Milton didn't always remember that witches were real anymore, and I didn't relish repeating the conversation with him over and over every time he caught me in the act.

A little levitation off the top of a stepstool I could make seem natural, if the witnesses' eyes weren't directed to my feet.

Which, I supposed, they hadn't been in this case. *There's one blessing.*

"I'm Cable Woodward," the man said out of the blue as he extended a hand toward me. His cheeks darkened and he moved the hand smoothly back across the back of his short, wavy hair. "Milton's nephew. Oh. Guess you have your hands full."

Right. The game.

"Dahlia," I said by way of answer. I let out a sneeze. The dust up here was really getting to me. "Dahlia Poplar."

"*Gesundheit*, Dahlia." He offered me that dazzling little half-smile again, along with a handkerchief he pulled out of his shirt pocket.

I thanked him and took the crisp, white handkerchief, juggling the game in one hand and patting my nose with the other. It gave me a chance to study him closer, to search for the resemblance. Milton talked a lot about his sister, Ingrid, who'd moved away as a young adult, long before I'd been born.

He sometimes talked about her as if she were just upstairs—other times, he remembered that she'd "gone off on an adventure."

It'd been ages since he'd spoken about her normally, but I did remember him and his wife, Leana, talking about a nephew back in the day. *"We have a nephew about your age!" "I hope you can meet our nephew when he comes to visit." "I guess Ingrid couldn't make it this year. She and Craigle are exploring a rainforest!"*

Yes, for some reason, my childhood brain remembered their nephew's name as "Craigle." I supposed I'd thought it was a strange nickname for "Craig" or they were saying "Craig'll." *"Craig'll be there"* must have been "Cable'll be there" all along.

Cable, huh?

I went to hand him the handkerchief and hurriedly took it back again. Who handed someone a dirty handkerchief they'd just borrowed? I tucked it into a pouch on my golden belt, thankful the loops weren't full of potion flasks I'd have to explain. "The famous Craig—Cable Woodward here at last." It felt awfully hot in this small, cramped attic. The dusty memories packing the shelves all the way to the ceiling seemed to make the small space even more cramped and confining.

Cable chuckled. "Famous, huh?" His nose wrinkled. "Craig?"

"I might have gotten the name wrong. They kept talking about you, but you never showed."

"Not often, no," said Cable. My mind raced to

remember him ever visiting, but it came up blank. "Mom and I traveled a lot, rarely made it back to the States. And then I got my doctorate in England." He rubbed the back of his head some more. "I'm sorry I missed Aunt Leana's funeral. I've been teaching abroad for a few years in Scotland. I couldn't easily make it back."

Scotland. Across an ocean. After a lifetime of traveling all around the globe. He had the slightest tinges of an unplaceable accent, but it was more like a mixture of everything had sieved through his smooth Midwestern standard through time, leaving just traces behind.

I was suddenly irrationally jealous of the fact that he'd *traveled*, that he'd *lived* in places I'd just read about, had only seen on TV. Everywhere else in the world seemed like a fairy-tale setting to me.

"I'm the only nephew either of them had," he said, his elbow knocking up against a newer box labeled "Leana's clothes," kicking up a bit of dust into the air. He scrambled to stop it from sliding off the shelf. "They didn't have kids themselves and my mom is getting on in years—she had me rather later in life, you see—so I figured I was the only one who could really check in on Uncle Milton." He straightened his loosened tie. "So when I was offered a sabbatical for the semester, I decided I'd move in with him."

Move. In. With. Him?

Here?

To Luna Lane?

To this sleepy town where everyone knew to keep quiet about the fact that the paranormal exists, to watch what they said and did in front of visitors who might waltz right out of here someday and share the news with the world?

My heart sunk. And of course, I would be the one who'd have to be most careful.

As the last witch in town, that meant I couldn't perform magic where Mr. Here-for-a-Sabbatical-Semester might see it.

Not for half a year.

Not even to help me cheat just a little to perform my good deeds.

I winced, focusing on the sharp sting of the latest scale on my arm of shame.

He watched me so earnestly, so clearly worried that I had hurt myself during this little debacle.

And boy, did his dark eyes light up stunningly when clouded with concern.

This was going to be *a long* few months.

Chapter Two

*W*ell, what was done was done.

It wasn't like I was going to let a good deed go unfinished just because the sun had set. I didn't need a curse to actually enjoy helping people.

Heading for the drop-down ladder leading back to the second floor of Milton's house, I realized I had two choices: Toss that game down and hope it didn't come open and spread all of its contents all over the place on impact or use a little levitation magic to finesse it down gently. The curse business was over for the day, so I could have zapped the game straight into Milton's hands if I'd wanted.

Only I couldn't do that with Cable watching.

Down below, leaning up against the wall next to Milton's former bedroom, was Broomhilde, or as I more often called her, "Broomie."

My enchanted broomstick started shaking at the sight of me, eager to fly up and give me a lift.

Leaning on my knees over the open attic hatch, I poked my head through. "Stay," I hissed quietly, harsher than I'd intended.

Broomie cowed down below, bending her bristles as if hanging her head low.

"Careful!" Cable sauntered up beside me and started climbing down the ladder. "Here. Why don't you hand it down to me?"

Right. There was that option, too.

Wincing, I stretched my arm and cracked the newly-stoned flesh as I handed it down to Cable's waiting arms below. His eyebrows furrowed as he grabbed the game from me. "That looks like it might be infected. Did you get it recently?"

There was no tattoo parlor in town. But then again, I couldn't really explain that I'd never set foot outside of town limits, either.

"Yeah," I said. Not a lie. Shimmying down the stairs, I landed with a thud on both feet. Broomie got excited again and I had to dash over to take her in both hands, her knotty cedar branch shaft rubbing up against my fingers as she attempted to get free of my grip. "Still," I whispered, Broomie's rough twig brush scratching across my lips. "*LLITS*," I said even stronger, knowing the backward word would inject magic into the command.

Broomie went quite still in my hands, her form still crackling with energy that had no place to go.

15

I'd make it up to her later.

"Are you okay?" Cable pinched his chin with his free hand as he examined me.

Me with my face full of broom bristles, speaking under my breath in tongues.

I really had no practice when it came to keeping Luna Lane's secrets.

"Peachy," I answered. The flush crawling up my neck couldn't be just from the attic heat. Besides, the cooler air down here was doing wonders to relieve me. "Um, so why don't I take that to your uncle and you get the attic sealed up again?" Leaving no room for argument, I snatched the board game from his grip and dragged both the game and Broomie downstairs.

At the bottom of the stairs was a removable gate, latched so Milton wouldn't wander up there when in one of his episodes and take a tumble. I was glad to see Cable had taken care to set it up and latch it behind him after he'd ascended the stairs.

But as long as he wasn't looking…

I nodded my head toward the latch. "*NEPO*." It popped open.

I'd let Cable latch it behind me again.

Wandering down the hallway, I headed into the living room that had been converted to Milton's new bedroom since his illness had progressed. It was across the hall from a full bathroom, with easy access to the kitchen, though much of what was in there had safety locks, too, so Milton wouldn't hurt himself trying to make toast or frying an egg.

His queen-sized bed had been moved into the living room—a piece of cake with a witch around— and it took up one corner of the room near the sliding glass door overlooking his backyard. A nightstand beside the bedframe held a lamp and a faded, framed photograph of his wedding to Leana. Beside that was a photo taken several decades later, after my mom had moved to town. Mom and Leana were both bending over laughing, my little toddler self in front of them, blueberry pie spread all over my face. Though Leana had been a couple of decades older than my mom, they'd really been good friends, Leana almost like a young grandmother to me.

Losing Leana had hit me hard for a while— she'd been there for me when I'd lost my mom. She'd been almost as devastated as I'd been.

Milton's small TV hung on the wall over his dresser across the way, tuned to a black-and-white movie from earlier days. A recliner offered him the option of watching from a chair, but he usually just sat up in bed.

Right now, Milton sat at the edge of the bed, staring off into space until I stepped into the room.

Sometimes I wished there were more people his age in town. More contemporaries to keep him company. But Doc Day was the second-oldest human Luna Lane resident, and she was a good fifteen years younger than Milton.

Milton was the last of his generation now. The last to stick it out in Luna Lane until retirement.

But we all kept him company. And he didn't even remember he was old half the time regardless.

"You found it!" Milton practically squealed, coming to life.

"Yes, it was quite hidden away," I said, leaning Broomie against the foot of his bed. "ESAELER," I said to her quietly, and she shuddered back to life. Her bristles whapped once like a woman flinging her hair over her shoulders, and I tossed my free hand up in the air. "There's an outsider here," I explained. "Didn't you see him?" In the hallway, the creak of the attic trap door slamming shut above us preceded the shuffle of soft footfalls down the steps and the release of the gate at the bottom.

"Let's play the game," said Milton, clapping his hands together. "We have to win the game."

Broomie went stiffly still. So she understood now at least.

"Uncle Milton, your robe is on backward," said Cable.

So it was. He must have put it on after he'd sent me off to look for the game. It was just after sunset, but Milton always liked to turn in early. Faine would be by with his supper from Hungry Like a Pup soon. Between half the town looking in on him and frequent home visits from Doc Day, Milton usually managed without a live-in nephew there to peel him out of his robe and help him slide it back on correctly. Still, it was kind of sweet to see. Milton still wore his checkered button-down shirt underneath, though he'd managed to put on his striped pajama bottoms.

"I'm fine, I'm fine." Milton waved Cable away as his nephew began to fuss over his robe belt. His robe still open, the material swishing around him, Milton hobbled over to me, his eyes drawn to the dusty box in my hand. "Leana, I'll play. I promise I'll play. You were right. We just played it *wrong*. Has to be." His eyes went glassy. "You found it," he said again, this time almost in awe.

"Uh, yeah," I repeated. I handed him the box—though not before turning to the side and blowing some more dust off its surface—and went to drag the vintage, green square card table he usually had his meals on closer to him.

Gray, wispy hairs stuck out this way and that atop Milton's balding head, his lined, dark peach skin speckled with age spots. He didn't wear glasses—his vision was good despite his age—but there was an eyeglasses chain around his neck anyway, his wife's reading glasses draped from them. He wore those for comfort more than necessity.

White, wiry follicles sprouted out from his ears and dotted the fingers that gripped the game in both hands so reverently. Hunched over and slightly swaying, he looked up and stared at Broomie in front of him.

"Do you think she'll want to play too?" he asked.

Sometimes he *did* remember all about the paranormal things going on in Luna Lane. And right now, he was remembering at the worst possible time.

"Leana can't play right now," I told him, a steady hand on his elbow to guide him to the folding table. It was fairly large; there would be plenty of room to lay out the box's contents if he so chose. "He often talks about her," I explained to Cable. I'd rather he think that than realize Milton was talking about my broomstick.

Though I supposed Cable might not think much about that coming from his uncle in this state, either.

"Leana," said Milton quietly. He put the box down on the tray and stared at it. "Leana can't play."

"Right," I said.

"And Jessmyn? Abraham?" he asked.

I didn't know who they were, but he'd mentioned them in the past few months before.

"They can't play, either," I said simply. It was kinder than arguing with him and upsetting him.

Milton sat down at the edge of his bed, his gaze still fixed on the box.

"But it's Saturday," he said. "Games Club."

"It's Sunday, Milton," I said. He didn't always remember the day of the week.

"Saturday is Games Club." Milton nodded.

Leana and Milton *had* played an awful lot of games together. I wondered if it had always been on Saturdays. But I'd have hardly called that a "Games Club."

"I know about Games Club," said Cable. He sat on the bed beside Milton and gave the elderly man a sideways hug. "Mom told me you and Leana would play games every Saturday with your neighbors, Jessmyn and Abraham Davis. But that was decades ago. Back when Mom still lived here—and I guess a while after."

"Neighbors?" I lived in the house next to Milton's now. Mom had moved in there shortly before I'd been born. She'd never told me the name of whomever she'd bought it from. She'd never even told me how she'd come to Luna Lane. She'd grow rather cagey about her "life before" anytime I'd asked, so I'd stopped asking.

"Oh, yeah, they had a standing date. Every Saturday, complete with a mini potluck and wine. Playing a different game each week, discussing movies, news, politics—whatever made an evening lively."

"Abraham doesn't know a good political policy from a warthog," muttered Milton.

Cable chuckled.

I couldn't picture local politics getting heated in Luna Lane. We had a mummy for a mayor and no one ever bothered to run against him. He been here since before the town had been founded.

"Still, he can play a heck of a game," said Milton, smiling. "He's good at bluffing. Maybe he should *go into* politics."

"Mom says he did, Milton," Cable said. "Abraham and Jessmyn moved away—he ran for state legislature in a bigger city. At least that's what you told her some years back. I don't know if he even won." Cable looked thoughtful.

Milton frowned as what his nephew had said made the gears in his brain start working. More often than not, it was easier to let him think whatever he wanted than to correct him like that. It wasn't like he would remember the information anyway.

"Abraham moved…?" asked Milton.

"What he means to say is Games Club can't meet today," I said quickly. I tilted my head, silently asking Cable to play along. "But how about we play with you tomorrow? Bring back the Games Club?" That could count as tomorrow's good deed, surely. Cheering up an old man.

Cable smiled. "Sure. We can be in Games Club now, Uncle Milton."

"Games Club meets on Saturdays." Milton frowned as his shaky hand caressed the game board box. The more I looked at it, the more obvious it was a Clue knockoff. Down to the murder suspects and the posh mansion.

The doorbell rang and I offered to get it, snatching up Broomie before heading down the hallway.

"Faine!" I said, my smile brightening.

Carrying a paper bag full of Milton's daily supper order from her restaurant downtown was Faine Vadas, my best friend since childhood. Chef extraordinaire. Class valedictorian. Genuine full-moon werewolf.

"What's this I hear about Milton having a visitor?" Faine asked by way of greeting as I opened the door. "Mayor Abdel said Ingrid had phoned ahead to let him know her son was coming to visit her brother. Just like him to forget to mention that until the guy was driving into town already."

Searing heat crawled up my neck. *Thanks for the warning, Mr. Mayor.* "Yup. His nephew. Here for *the rest of the year.* As normal as normal comes."

"Oh. That's a shame." Faine's nose wrinkled and I knew she got what I was saying.

"Hi," called Cable as he emerged from down the hall.

Faine's dark brown eyes bulged. She put a hand on her pear-shaped hip, her outfit, as usual, a stunning vintage-style dress, this one popping in green against her pale complexion. Her curly, brown hair hung over one shoulder. "I don't know if I'd call *that* normal," she whispered. "More like holy moly."

I elbowed her playfully. "Cable, this is Faine Vadas. She and her *husband* own the local diner."

"Hungry Like a Pup?" A smirk danced on Cable's lips.

"That's the one." She held the bag up. "And I'm here with Milton's pastrami on rye and chicken and wild rice soup. I brought some extra when I heard you were coming, if you'd like. First time's free!"

"Well, they *do* say news travels fast in small towns." Cable laughed. "Thank you. That's most generous of you."

"Welcome to Luna Lane," crooned Faine. "And swing by the diner, connected to the pub. We don't bite." Her incisor gleamed just a little as her lips curled. "Well, we *try* not to."

Cable offered up a bemused smile.

He had no idea she wasn't kidding.

Chapter Three

*T*he new scale did itch something fierce. There was no anti-itch enchantment I could cast with a backward word that I knew of, at least not one that *I* had the power to cast, so I'd have to mix together a potion.

Or just get some healing ointment from Vogel's.

Just across the street from Milton's and my houses—I noticed the new car in Milton's driveway now, an almost comically small tan two-seater—was the town's general store, run for several generations by Milton's own family. The last name had belonged to his maternal grandfather.

He'd had no kids and "Craigle" hadn't been interested in taking over, so for most of my life, it had been run by Goldie and Arjun Mahajan.

Goldie had liked to tease us as kids that there was an *apsara* in her family, but no, they were just normal, everyday humans. Just the kind who was living in a town about a quarter full of paranormal creatures. We couldn't be wall-to-wall supernatural. Not with Amazon delivery and a Starbucks just thirty miles outside of town.

Not that I'd ever been there. But Faine had brought me some cappuccinos-to-go on occasion. Truth be told, she brewed better.

Broomie vibrated in my hand as we approached the front door. "I know, I know," I told her. "Cornhusks." She always wanted cornhusks. It was all she could eat.

"Dahlia, darling!" said Goldie as I stepped through the door to the cacophony of overhead jingling bells. She was in the middle of tearing down the front window display and stacking up cans of soup along with cutouts of red and orange leaves. I could help with that, but she liked to do the work herself and when she did accept my help, she only ever let me help the old-fashioned way to help with my curse.

"There's a handsome new man in town. Jeremiah saw him drive in," said Arjun before even saying, "Hello."

"So everyone keeps pointing out." A sigh escaped my lips. "He's a normie, Arjun."

"And so are we," said Goldie, wiping her hands on her apron. Her long, dark hair was pulled back into a bun, the colorful pink silk saree she wore beneath the white Vogel's apron bringing a radiance to her oak brown skin. The fabric clung softly to every bit of her plump, apple-shaped body in the height of comfort and style.

"So are our sons," added Arjun, a twinkle in his hazel brown eye. His black hair was half-faded to white, the temples pulling back just a bit to give him a widow's peak. His dark hands rested across his round belly, his own Vogel's apron hanging across khakis and a baby-blue collared shirt.

"So we know why she never would marry either of them," said Goldie, tapping her husband across the chest with the back of her hand. "They're *normies.*"

"*Goldie,*" I said as Broomie leaped from my grip and headed straight for the fresh vegetables. "I didn't marry either because they were my friends. And they left town. And they both married other people."

"I'm only teasing you," said Goldie. "Broomhilde, you know not to make a mess! Broomhilde!" She chased after Broomie, who'd already stuck her bristles deep within the discard can full of cornhusks.

"Sorry," I said, wincing.

Arjun just chuckled. "What do you need today, Dahlia? Something *normal* or something a little more special?"

"Maybe a little of both," I admitted. I pulled

out a scribbled list from the pouch at my waist, my folded-up shopping tote and Cable's handkerchief coming with it. "NAELC," I said with a wave of my hand at the handkerchief, tote, and paper. Arjun watched curiously but said nothing. He'd seen my magic almost every day. If only I could have done that earlier, I could have handed the borrowed handkerchief straight back to Cable. For now, I slipped the kerchief and its red-monogramed "CW" back inside the pouch.

The black, short-sleeved dress I wore was simple and flowy, but the golden belt with the pouch and the currently empty little bands for small vials of potion as needed was all business. "Some groceries and…" Laying out the unfurled tote on the counter and handing Arjun the list, I showed him my left arm, the pink skin stinging something fierce around the new stone scale.

Arjun clucked his tongue. "You didn't do your good deed in time?"

"*What?*" called Goldie from across the store. She held Broomie in her arms, the broomstick curled up like a cat—she was flexible that way. Broomie was chomping on husks, the yellow, leafy things disappearing into her mess of twiggy brush bristles. "Dahlia, darling, why didn't you come to us?"

"I appreciate that. You know I do. But it was totally my fault. A mistake." I couldn't quite meet her gaze. "It won't happen again."

"What *did* happen?" asked Arjun.

"It was my turn to keep Milton company, and I thought I could do something for him. I just... kind of got wrapped up in a theory on how to break the curse today and I left a *little bit* late and then the good deed took a *little bit* longer than I anticipated and—"

Goldie reached out to put a finger to my lips. "No excuses."

"I know." Sighing, I opened my arms outward for Broomie to hop over. She did, letting out a little gurgle as the last of the husks disappeared into her ill-defined maw. "Sorry about the mess," I added. "YDIT," I said toward the vegetable section, waving a single hand. The scattered bits of cornhusks all over the floor and the nearby display flew right back into the bin.

Goldie waved me off. "You know she's always welcome to our cornhusks. They'll just go in the garbage anyway."

Broomie's brush head shot up at that. I pet her to soothe her, the twigs of her bristles poking against my fingertips. "You can't eat that much at once," I reminded her.

Annoyed, she slapped the very tip of her handle against my forearm like a cat whapping its tail.

I winced. The new scale was still tender.

"Let's get you some healing ointment," said Arjun, stepping out from behind the counter.

Goldie talked to me about her day as Arjun gathered the items from my list. You *could* shop by yourself at the store, but they both seemed to prefer this arrangement.

"Doc Day is back from visiting her grandkids," she said. "Said she'd swing by in the morning to check on Milton. How *is* Milton?"

"Fine, I suppose. I'm not sure he even knows who his nephew is. But he doesn't seem to mind him being there."

"I'll feel so much better knowing someone's there to look out for him." Goldie fanned her fingers across her chest. "It's been hard on him since Leana died."

"Yeah…" She'd done it all by herself before then, hardly allowing anyone in town to do more than send a casserole once in a while. It was sad to think Milton didn't even fully understand enough to miss her.

"And how did you find this mysterious *normal* stranger?" She batted her eyelashes.

"By falling into his arms," I blurted out.

It was the truth.

Goldie burst out laughing. "*This* I have to hear!"

It would have to wait, though. The front door opened, the overhead bell jingling, and in stepped the normie man himself.

Broomie's head shot up and she reacted in a snap, curling outward like an inanimate broom and leaning against the counter with a clatter.

"Hello," said Goldie, all smoothness. She stepped past me to block Cable's view of my broom and held out her hand to the professor, who practically towered over her. "You must be Milton's nephew."

"Is *everyone* here so friendly?" asked Cable, taking her hand. "You must be Goldie and Arjun. Mom told me you'd taken over the family business. And brought it into the twenty-first century."

Goldie pressed her fingers to her lips. "Oh, nothing so amazing. We're honored Milton chose to sell."

"This should be everything," said Arjun, putting a basket down filled to the brim with fruits, vegetables, flour, cereal, and every other snack I could think of. There were a few extra cornhusks tucked away at the edges and a jar of healing ointment on top. Underneath it all were likely the tinctures and essential oils for which I'd asked for my potions. He started ringing it all up on the electronic register. Truth be told, that felt like the only update they'd made to fit in to the modern century. Not that anyone in Luna Lane would be complaining.

"What can we get for you, young fellow?" asked Arjun as he bagged my lettuce. Broomie twitched just slightly at the sight of the husks about to go into the cloth tote.

Cable fumbled for his wallet, which he kept in his back pocket. "Oh, uh, I guess some basics I forgot to pack. Toothbrush, aftershave, that sort of thing."

"Those are some *very* basics," said Goldie,

wagging her finger at him. "Never travel without a toothbrush, son. Looks like the two of you are both in need of some lecturing today." Cable raised a brow as he looked me over. I chose to focus on the counter instead. "Did you remember to pack your briefs or boxers?" asked Goldie, nonplussed. "My sons always forgot to pack their tighty—"

"*Goldie*," I hissed. But I just stared up at Cable, the tips of his ears turning bright red.

"I think I did forget those," he said, his voice suddenly weakened.

I stared. And then I laughed. We all laughed, Cable cringing but chuckling all the same.

"You will have to go to the tailor's," said Goldie.

"Or order from Amazon," added Arjun.

Goldie smacked him across the chest. "Do not encourage mail order here."

"Online ordering," said Arjun, sliding some of my tincture bottles inside the tote. "Twenty-first century, remember?"

"Yes, yes," said Goldie.

"I guess I'll see what my uncle has," mumbled Cable. "It's getting a bit late, and I know stores in a town this small don't usually stay open long past sundown."

"Oh, don't be silly," said Goldie. "I can call Spindra up."

"Spindra?" Cable asked. The name *was* rather on the nose.

"She's nocturnal."

She was also a spiderwoman, but I was glad Goldie had managed to leave that part out, as strange as "being nocturnal" might have been.

"A night owl," I said quickly.

"More like a night arachnid," said Arjun with a chuckle.

I slapped a palm across my face.

"Thank you, Arjun." I took hold of the tote and slid it up my arm. "How much do I owe you?" I reached for the pouch at my waist. But it only held Cable's handkerchief. Right.

I fished it out. "Let me give this back to you."

Cable seemed caught unawares, ignoring me for a second too long until he scrambled to take his property back from me. He looked it over, unfolding it. It was crisp white, perfectly wrinkle-free. "You cleaned *that* fast. I think it's in better shape than it was the day Mom gave it to me."

My heart thundered. I *had* cleaned it supernaturally fast, my magic doing a better job on it than a washing machine could have. I'd only just left Milton's.

Foolish, foolish Dahlia.

"Baking soda," I mumbled, as if that would explain it all. Swallowing, I patted my pouch again, but there was no money. I'd left in such a hurry before sundown, I'd forgotten to conjure up some more cash from Mom's small fortune she'd moved into town with. Wherever she'd gotten it, I didn't know, but she'd kept it in between dimensions, safely tucked away.

"On your tab is fine," Arjun said, knowing I was good for it. His eyes sparkled with amusement over my exchange with Cable. I was glad *one* of us was amused.

But I couldn't help but be grateful. If there was one good thing about being stuck in a small town, it was the fact that I at least didn't have to worry about cobbling together a few odd jobs to pay the bills.

No, I just had to do odd jobs to save my hide. In more ways than one.

"Thank you," I said, grabbing hold of Broomhilde.

"Let me show you the toiletries," said Goldie, taking Cable by the arm, as if he were her escort. He smirked but allowed himself to be shown the way, tucking his handkerchief back in his front pocket. "And then I'll call up Spindra for you."

"Thank you so much, Miss Goldie," said Cable. I reached for the door handle.

"'Goldie' is fine, please."

"Of course. Say, Goldie, I almost forgot. Uncle Milton asked if you'd pick up some…" He paused a moment, and I grew still, waiting for the witchy instinct of dread weighing down my gut to make sense. "Facial powder?" he said at last. "For someone named Virginia? Who's Virginia? Or is she long gone, too?"

He wasn't too far off with that one.

At the mention of the town ghost's name, the store went so quiet, you could hear a pin drop.

Or a broomstick munching on the cornhusks she'd filched out of my tote bag.

Chapter Four

I left Goldie and Arjun to explain away Virginia. It was simple enough to make up a small lie or feign ignorance.

It was less simple to explain a ghost if she was hanging around Milton, feeding him shopping list items his normie nephew was supposed to pick up for her.

"NEPO," I said to my front door, and it opened. It hadn't been locked, but this saved me the trouble of turning the handle. I didn't need security measures in Luna Lane. Besides, the cozy brick cottage was overrun with vines and brambles. I liked my yard a little chaotic.

The place might have seemed abandoned to the passerby. But it went with the witchy ambiance, if fairy tales were anything to go off of.

I tossed the tote on the nearby island that separated the great room from the kitchen. Down the hall were two bedrooms and a bathroom. Simple, quaint, and ideal for a witch who didn't want to waste a lot of time casting enchantments to keep a large place tidy.

Broomie flew off straightaway into her wicker pet bed, the last of the husks devoured and it being long past time for a nap. Before we'd headed over to Milton's, we'd been flying around the woods surrounding Luna Lane—almost as far as I could go before the curse pulled me backward—scouring for potion ingredients. We hadn't had much luck.

I never had much luck when it came to discovering a solution to my lifelong problem.

Shoving aside the flasks, I picked up the miniature cast-iron cauldron, putting it back near the unlit stone fireplace. Inside sloshed the riverwood sap and the petals of a budding bloom at dawn I'd started a recipe with. The ingredients would go bad before I had a chance to try again. If this "Potion to Improve One's Comforts" was even the solution.

"I'd sure be more *comfortable* not having to perform a good deed every day and being able to leave town, wouldn't I?" I said out loud. Broomie was sleeping now, a steady rhythmic purring coming from her bed, so I was talking to myself.

I flipped through the open potions book and sighed. It was highly doubtful this was the one. But it was page 298 of 781, and I had zeroed in on all the most obvious possibilities from the start. Now I was down to painstakingly getting through each solution page by page until *something* helped me.

The ingredients I'd asked Arjun for were part of tomorrow's potion. But I hadn't even finished this one.

They would have to wait.

Tidying up the rest of my workspace, I pushed back the table to expose the full rune circle my mom had scratched on the hardwood floor long ago, the one I maintained whenever a line started fading or a clump of dust threatened to send the circle's magic out of whack.

Usually, Ginny wasn't that hard to find.

But I didn't have time to play her games, whatever they might have been.

Rolling my shoulders, I stared down at the circle. There were stars and blooms and other shapes carved at just the right angles along the trajectory of the sun overhead. Not that I often let any sunlight in here. It pulled focus, redirecting the room's flow of energy.

I opened my mouth to perform the enchantment, then realized I was missing something. Darting to the coatrack beside my front door, I grabbed my pointed, black hat, which had a purple belt as an accent.

A witch's hat grounded the magical energy floating all around her, funneling it right into her gray matter.

"Okay," I said, raising my hands over the edge of the rune circle.

"AINIGRIV, EMOC!"

Ginny wasn't hard to conjure. Since she was always floating somewhere in town, it was just a matter of yanking her here, where I wanted her, rather than channeling any energy across the borders of life and the afterlife.

The specter who cheerfully haunted Luna Lane spun in a shot of bright light at the center of my rune circle, the shapes carved into the floor glowing with a jaunty energy.

Virginia Kincaid, forever-twenty-one, floated a few inches off the ground in front of me. Her ghastly white glow muted her color, but when she felt like it, she could show off a mess of straw-colored hair she wore in a bun beneath her broad white hat. Her long, brown skirt reached her ankles, with long sleeves and a high collar shirtwaist blouse buttoned just beneath her chin—leaving *everything* to the imagination. The ruffles on her cream-colored blouse were punctuated by a red, ruby broach, and if the mood suited her, she'd appear with a frilly lace parasol, protecting her inhumanly pale skin from imagined sun damage.

"You could have just sent a calling card," she said, fluffing the puffy material over her shoulders.

"Sure. I'll go out of my way to leave a calling card with the butler you don't have at a house that's no longer standing rather than summoning you directly."

"Well, what am I supposed to do? You know as well as I that my house burned down. How else do you explain the fact that I died in my prime?" She gestured to her whole body. "Never even got married, and I had a young man who was courting me. I thought we were…" She sniffled. "But that was all long before your time, Miss Poplar." She stuck her button nose up in the air. "My home's a bowling alley now."

"It's nothing now. The bowling alley closed years ago," I pointed out. None of this was news to me. Almost as long as I could remember her flitting about town when I'd been a child, she'd told anyone who would listen her tale of woe.

She deserved my sympathy, of course, but she needed some for the rest of us. *She* didn't have anything left to lose if she messed up and let Cable see her.

"Have you been bothering Milton?" I asked.

"Of course not. *Bother*," she repeated. "Really, Miss Poplar. I thought we were friends!"

"We are," I said quickly. But memories of every time she'd just *shown up* uninvited during gab sessions with Faine, good deeds I was trying to focus on, and even dates with… Well. She'd latched on to me almost immediately after she'd introduced herself to me back when I'd been about ten, spending more time with me than anyone else in town. Or so it had seemed to me, I supposed. She'd seemed older, sophisticated then. But I'd aged twenty years and in that time, every irritating aspect of her perpetual immaturity had grown stronger and stronger in my head.

Still. She was a ghost. She'd died. A little sympathy.

I took a deep breath. "But you know Milton doesn't see things clearly anymore. You showing up could upset him."

"Nonsense," she said, crossing one ankle daintily over the other, her knees bent and her derriere protruding as if sitting on an invisible floating chair. "Mr. Woodward adores spending time with me. Unlike *some* of my friends, it seems." She sniffled and stared up above my head.

From the corner of the room, Broomie's soft snores punctuated the silence.

I let out a sigh. "Just be careful not to upset him."

"I *am*," she said in a flat voice.

She was waiting for me to assuage her. I didn't have time for pity parties.

"All right, but then you must have noticed he has a visitor."

Ginny brightened at that. "Why, of course. Luna Lane hasn't had such a handsome new resident since… Well, I might say since *ever*."

"You always told me Draven was the *most comely lad* you'd ever lain eyes on."

"Oh, Draven's last year's news." Her eyes sparkled with mischief. "As you keep telling me."

"More like five-years-ago news."

"Has it been that long? Time certainly does fly." She fanned herself with a ghostly lace glove she peeled off one of her hands.

"Yes, well, you can't date him," I pointed out. "He's a normie just here for a few months and you're…" I left the rest unsaid.

She looked affronted. "I would never dream of it! I was thinking of him for *a dear friend*." She probably meant me. I hoped she didn't mean me. "I may be *dead*, but I can still be a matchmaker."

"*No one* in town should date him." I put both hands on my hips, my voice strangely trembling as I spoke what should have been obvious to me. "He's *leaving* town in a few months. He's a normie. He can't know about"—I gestured at her, at my mess of witchy paraphernalia, at me—"strange things in Luna Lane."

"I see." Ginny nodded and slipped her glove back on.

"Just… be more careful around him and Milton, okay?"

"Of course," she said brightly.

"Okay." I cleared my throat. "So, I guess I need to clean this mess and make some supper. Then I want to study some more from my potions book before I go to bed."

"All right, all right, I can tell when I'm not wanted." Ginny's parasol appeared out from thin air. The sun wasn't even shining anymore, but that would make no difference to her either way. She headed for the door, another relic from life that she needn't have bothered with. She didn't even open it.

"You know, you needn't be so worried about *me* when I doubt the vampires will last two minutes around the handsome professor before making it *dreadfully* obvious what they are."

A chill ran down my spine as the two flasks in my hand clinked together. I'd been about to take them to the kitchen sink for scrubbing.

"So, anyway, I'll see you tomorrow for Games Club," she said quickly.

"What? Ginny—" I turned.

But she was already rushing through the door, leaving a grime of green ectoplasm dripping down the solid wood in her wake.

Chapter Five

*V*irginia the ghost may have been haughty and supercilious and stubborn and flirtatious and all manner of adjectives, but she was also right.

Despite being a sheer-white specter, she was hardly the showiest paranormal in town.

But they had to know the stakes.

No pun intended. I knew they tried to *avoid* stakes. Of a different nature.

Based on the rate of the news spreading around Luna Lane, Draven or one of his coven mates would surely have heard about him by now, even if they hadn't been awake yet when Cable had arrived. Their human daytime employees always did inventory with the vampires when the undead awoke. So they'd know. They'd have to know to behave.

But he was young, fresh blood...

Cursing to myself, I thought about grabbing Broomie and then decided to let her rest, the little rise and fall of her bristles warming my heart. Heading for the door, I slipped on my black shawl, which I took down from the coatrack. Then I hesitated and hung the witch hat back up.

A witch costume I might be able to explain. But as just one more oddity in a town of strange things, it might just be the final straw that made the whole picture click in Cable's head. And I wasn't going to be the one responsible for that. I'd already messed up with the handkerchief.

"ESOLC," I said to the door behind me, not bothering to lock it.

A simple lock wouldn't keep away the only real threat I'd ever known.

But Eithne Allaway, the witch who'd cursed me at birth, hadn't shown her face in Luna Lane since my mother's death.

I pushed all thoughts of her away. I didn't need more stress on top of this Cable situation right now.

Why wasn't anyone else stressed about Cable?

Leave it to the Luna Lane's resident conscripted do-gooder to look out for the town's best interests.

The chilly, autumn air caused me to pull my shawl tighter around my shoulders as I shuffled my feet down the sidewalk. The lights were out at Vogel's, so Arjun and Goldie must have gone home. Milton's dim bedside light was on in his living room window. He kept it on all night, so maybe that being

45

the only light on downstairs meant he'd gone to bed.

Upstairs in Milton's guest room another light was on. Good. Cable must have been settling in for the night. A flush crept onto my cheeks as I wondered if Spindra had gotten him some underwear. She might have been weaving it up from her own silks as I thought about it.

My heart beat faster. Okay, enough thinking about poor Cable's unmentionables.

Now I was sounding like Virginia.

It took another ten minutes before I reached downtown, the town's sole pub, First Taste, looming like a beacon in a row of otherwise-shuttered eclectic storefronts. Luna Lane closed with the sun, for the most part.

There were still lights on in the adjoining café, Hungry Like a Pup, but they were offering minimal lighting as Grady, Faine's husband, flipped the café seats up onto the tables to clean the floor. He spied me through the clear front window and waved, a broad, friendly smile on his dark brown face. I waved back. Around him, their three kids rushed around with mops, big sister seven-year old Flora already halfway as tall as her lithe father. Five-year-old Fauna copied her big sister's movements. Three-year-old Falcon, just barely visible in the window, toddled aimlessly behind them. All shared the same light brown complexion, the same coiled black hair that was like their father's. Fauna was easy to distinguish from her sister by the puffy pigtails, and the fact that she seemed to take after her shorter mother, as Flora had more than a head and a half on her.

I gripped the handle to First Taste's front door, the heavy wood and rarely oiled metal hinges creaking as I opened it in front of me.

It sounded for all the world like the entrance to a haunted house.

Inside, faint mist flew out from the corners of the dark bar, coating the entire place in a faintly smoky aesthetic.

Mayor Abdel was in a back booth in the corner, his three town hall human coworkers cheering as they all clinked together lagers overflowing with foam. Though he was wearing a dress shirt with rolled-up sleeves, Abdel had clean, white strips of cloth wrapped around his arms, hands, and most of his head, leaving very little of his face exposed. He was far from rotten in appearance— the magic imbued in his wrappings kept that from happening. But without them, he'd no longer be undead.

Okay. A kooky mayor who wrapped himself up in strips of white cloth. He could just be eccentric if Cable asked.

The music ringing out from the bar speakers overhead was eerie and ancient, complete with melodramatic rumblings of thunder that were punctuated with flickering low lights throughout the bar.

And this bar? Just a theme bar, I could say. Nothing but a bit of fun.

"Lia!" A raised bottle of beer over by the bar caught my attention. Sheriff Roan Birch, human resident of Luna Lane and our only lawperson.

I saddled over to him and slipped on the open stool beside him.

"I haven't seen you here in ages," said the sheriff, taking a slow, savoring sip from his bottle. He seemed cheerful, though tired, a slight slouch to his back. Maybe running the town's one-man police force was wearing on him as he neared retirement, even in a town as peaceful as Luna Lane.

"I had a need," I said, trying to flag down Ravana or Qarinah. At least Draven was nowhere to be seen at the moment.

"What are you having?" he asked. "I'm buying."

With a jolt to my stomach, I realized I *still* hadn't conjured up more cash. I was responsible for a lot of Luna Lane's good deeds. And for a lot of the open tabs, apparently.

"Just seltzer water," I said. "Thank you."

Roan caught Qarinah's attention as she sauntered back over from refilling the mayor's table's drinks and he relayed my order. She smiled brightly when he spoke to her, laughing along with him at some dad joke about not finding happiness at the bottom of the beer.

"Who's happy when the beer runs out?" he asked.

Qarinah playfully slapped his shoulder and spoke in a soft, accented voice. "Well, then, I promise to keep them coming."

"You do that, sweetheart." In the dim light of the spooky "theme bar," Roan's chuckling died off as he took a sip from his bottle and studied me. "What's gotten your goat today? Nothing too rough, or you wouldn't have just asked for seltzer."

I returned the studious glare. He was in his mid-fifties, had been a cornerstone of my life since before I could remember. Mom had raised me alone, but "Uncle Roan" had often swung by to make sure Mom had everything she'd needed. It was no secret in this small town that Roan had had a thing for my mom and her sunny disposition, but she'd never reciprocated. Though she'd cherished him dearly.

He'd been handsome enough once, though age hadn't been as kind to him as it had been to any of these immortals. Tan lines poked out of his officer's uniform, his brown-and-gray hair mussed flat from being under his hat all day long. He had a smart, trim moustache already half white, and he'd earned way more wrinkles than most people twice his age, as well as a bit of a gut. But he didn't let the slow character of Luna Lane's crime scene keep him totally sedentary. His arms were still pretty sculpted, and I knew he could bench-press with the best of them.

"Dahlia. You have not been here in… years,"

said Qarinah as she set my seltzer water down in front of me. She was gorgeous—as all vampires were. Her light brown complexion was a bit wan, and there were dark circles under her eyes, but otherwise, with the black hair that reached her waist, the perfectly curvy body, the striking, curved nose, and those dark, dark irises rimmed only slightly in red—she was worthy of superstardom, if only she could spend any time during the day outside of her coffin.

"I wanted to talk to you," I explained. Roan went quiet, observant. That was the lawman in him.

"Me?" Qarinah asked, putting her serving tray down on the counter.

"Well, you and Ravana. And…"

"Draven's in the back." She thumbed over her shoulder.

I shook my head quickly. "You two can tell him later." I could trust them to pass on the message.

Qarinah flagged Ravana over from the other end of the bar, where she was wiping down empty glasses, and Ravana's bright red lips parted into a wide smile, revealing her sharp incisors without a second thought.

This was why I'd wanted to speak to them.

"Miss Dahlia Poplar, setting foot in our bar." She fluffed her wavy, chestnut hair over one shoulder, putting a manicured hand on the hip of her red curve-hugging dress. Hers matched Qarinah's, though Qarinah wore violet instead. "To what do we owe the pleasure?"

She was ghastly pale. Closer to Virginia's complexion than even Faine's. Her violet, red-rimmed eyes sparkled as she spared both Roan and me a glance, her tongue trailing across one fang as if inspecting meat.

I shuddered. The three vampires in Luna Lane didn't drink anyone who didn't volunteer—and they certainly didn't drink them dry. But Ravana always made me feel like she was one sudden move away from breaking the pact that had been a condition of their moving here all those many years ago.

"We have a visitor in town," I said.

"We know." Ravana ran her fingers across her long neck. "Quite a tasty snack, I hear tell."

"Ravana." Qarinah nudged her with her hip. "You're scaring her."

She was?

Yes, judging by the tremble in my knee, she was.

"Dahlia knows I'm only joking," said Ravana with a wink. "What I really meant was he's quite handsome, is he not?"

I opened my mouth and shut it. Roan quirked an eyebrow, and I knew—I just *knew*—he was making some mental note, doing some "observation" of me. Well, he was way off-track if he thought I had any strong opinions on Cable in any way.

Way off-track, I reminded myself.

"Sure," I said, twirling a lock of orange hair around my finger. "But that's not the issue at hand."

"I think Draven would very much argue that's an issue," said Ravana, her voice sultry and low.

"Because he can't stand a little competition?" I asked dryly, thinking of his status as the town's most handsome—and eligible—bachelor. Two hundred years and counting. Not counting the two hundred he'd spent in Europe after turning.

"Not for *you*," said Ravana. "Draven will get pouty."

My throat went dry, but Ravana's eyes lit up mischievously. She was just teasing me.

Surely, she was just teasing me. I was one little blip in Draven's long, long, *long* history. And I didn't exactly have fond memories of all the preening.

"Who's pouty?"

The sound of his trademark heavy-heeled leather boots across the floor pricked at my ears even before he'd spoken.

"Why, you, of course, Draven, darling." Ravana trailed two fingers up Draven's broad shoulder as he stepped up beside her. "As you always are," she cooed, pinching his cheek as if he were a chubby baby.

Draven was not amused, but he didn't bat her away. She slid past him and went to take an order. Jeremiah, the middle-aged farmer from just outside town who was responsible for much of Luna Lane's fresh market produce, lapped up the attention.

"You're back. In my bar," said Draven, as if nothing Ravana had done mattered.

He glared at me, his arm crossed over his lithe but sculpted chest. He wore a black leather jacket with no shirt underneath, the collar dipping down across his hairless pecs. He'd matched them with tight-fitting black leather pants, decorated with small chains protruding from the multiple pockets. His long, golden hair practically shone as it tumbled over his shoulders.

He, too, was snow-white pale, his steel gray eyes rimmed with red, his lips far too red to be natural.

My heart skipped a beat in his presence. He was good-looking. And, unfortunately, he knew it.

"Don't get too excited," I muttered. It wasn't like I hadn't seen him at all in the past five years. It was a small town. But it *did* help that he couldn't walk around during the daylight hours and most of the town shut down when he creaked open his coffin and joined the land of the living. With those narrow possibilities of crossing paths—even if he did own the bar connected to my best friend's café—it was simply a matter of a little magic here, a little magic there, and I could enchant myself out of his line of sight.

"*Excited* isn't the word I'd use to describe this." He gestured to himself and flung his head, swishing his hair.

Roan snorted into his almost empty bottle, the sound echoing like a musical jug.

"Let me get you another," said Qarinah.

"Anyway." I stared intently on the glass I held tightly between my hands. "Ravana walked off before I could finish saying… Well, Milton's nephew is in town, and he's only staying a few months."

Qarinah plopped another beer before Roan, popping the cap off and taking his empty bottle.

"And I should care because…?" Draven asked.

"Because he's a normie," I said, grinding my teeth together. "A human."

"Jeremiah's a *human*," said Draven. He tossed his hand out, pointing out the person attached to each name as he spoke. "And so is Chione. And Ryan. And Erik."

"Yeah, and they all live in Luna Lane," I said. "They're all one of us."

"They're all bloodbags. That's what humans are so good for. No offense, Roan." Draven nodded at him.

"If blood tastes as good to you as a cold brew does to me, I don't mind." Roan shrugged and took a swig of his beer. Qarinah giggled.

"Bloodbags" was what the vampires called the people who voluntarily let them drink their blood— just enough to sustain them. Not enough to turn the humans into new vampires, of course. But also not enough to drive them blood mad. That was when a normie's addiction to vampire venom got so bad, they lost all sense of control. It was a fine line, drinking just the right amount to not affect the human volunteer.

The door leading to Hungry Like a Pup opened, the dim light streaming into the dark pub, the door blocking my view of the restaurant. Probably Faine or Grady asking if the pub needed any more bar snacks before they went home. Otherwise, Faine's kitchens were closed, unfortunately. I was long overdue for supper. Ravana went to the door and said something. Above the riotous laughter spilling over from Mayor Abdel's table, I caught Ravana saying, "Not tonight," but that was it. She shut the door gently, her eyes trained downward the whole while, and picked up a rag to wipe down the opposite end of the counter. I clutched my glass of seltzer as I watched her. She'd seemed almost *too* sweet in her interaction just then, but Ravana was capricious like that.

Draven growled. "All this talk about blood... Darn it, Dahlia, you're making me ravenous." The way he gave me a onceover, I had no doubt it was *my* blood he was after.

"That's exactly what I mean," I said, withdrawing my hands from my glass and clutching my thighs. "Don't act like that in front of Cable."

"*Cable*?" Draven's nose wrinkled. "Is he an e-lec-tro-nic accessory?" He pronounced "electronic" slowly, enunciating each syllable as if the concept were foreign to him. He was still getting a bit used to modern innovations, I supposed. And Luna Lane wasn't exactly known for being at the forefront of technology.

"Har, har," I said, sliding off my stool. Screwing up my courage, I clenched my hands at my sides and stared Draven down. "No funny business around Cable. He plans to leave town one day, and he just doesn't need to know about us."

Draven thumbed his nose at me. "About *us*, us"—he pointed back and forth between him and me—"or us?" He gestured around him.

A wave of laughter echoed out in the bar. Ravana had moved over to the mayor's table, her tongue poking at her protruded incisor as she stood with her hand on the back of the booth behind Mayor Abdel, sizing up the town hall employees seated around him.

Apparently, they were dinner tonight.

"Neither," I snapped, turning to Roan and doing my best not to watch Draven out of the corner of my eye. "Thank you so much, Sheriff. Nice seeing you."

"Likewise." Roan tipped his beer bottle at me. "Now go home and relax. Stop stressing so much about the town and start thinking about just Lia for a change."

If only it were that simple.

Luna Lane needed me. And I needed Luna Lane.

My arm itched. I'd forgotten to apply the healing ointment Arjun had sent me home with.

"Is that a new scale there?" asked Draven. If I didn't know better, he might have sounded concerned.

"Yes," I said simply, and before he could reply with some *biting* remark, I headed out the door and put the chill and the mist of First Taste behind me.

Chapter Six

I had a restless night. I kept dreaming about good times with Draven, but they would warp into horrid nightmares. I curled up under his arm, breathing in the stark, leather scent of him as we watched the sky for shooting stars. But then I'd look up and he'd open his jaw wide, about to fit my entire head in his mouth, hissing as those fangs grew longer.

I shot up in bed at that last image. Draven had been rather self-focused during our time together, but he'd never been *that*. He'd never hurt me, had only bit me once and with my permission.

I scratched my throat absentmindedly, remembering the time he'd drunk my blood. There were no puncture marks now. Enchantments had taken care of that.

Though that reminded me, I didn't usually go around enchanting away the evidence of vampires partaking in the blood running through the veins of Luna Lane's citizens. Hopefully, Cable didn't take a good look at any bloodbag's neck in the next few months and wonder about the dual puncture scars. Maybe they'd all let me enchant away the evidence from now on.

After each and every session of feeding.

Massaging my temples, I realized I had a lot on my plate if I was going to keep Cable from ever finding out about us.

It might have been easier to spend more time with him, to enchant away any suspicious activity when he wasn't looking.

Though it wasn't like *that* would be suspicious at all, either.

Sighing, I got out of bed, petting Broomhilde where she lay sleeping stretched out across the bottom of the mattress, two clumps of her bristles spread out above her, almost like a cat's stretched-out legs.

Time to get going. The good deed today would provide an excuse for looking in on Cable.

My stomach growled.

But first... breakfast.

I enchanted myself clean—I hardly ever used the shower—and got dressed for the day, wearing a plain purple dress much like my basic black one and affixing my belt in place. Out of habit, I reached for my pointed hat on the way out but thought again, instead wrapping my black shawl around my arms and heading outside. I didn't bother to lock the door again, waving to Goldie as she swept out front of Vogel's.

I ate almost all of my breakfasts at my best friend's. This one would be all the sweeter since I'd gone to bed in a sour mood last night, the seltzer water my only sustenance for the evening.

The scent of cinnamon rolls hit my nostrils the moment I walked inside the café.

"That smells delicious!" I called out, not caring who heard me. Everyone in town was like family in some way. Maybe some just like distant cousins, but—

"Dahlia! How's the ankle? The tattoo?"

I stilled. Beside me, at *my* usual table, was Cable, a warm cinnamon roll on a plate in front of him and a steaming mug of coffee in his hand.

"Oh. Hi," I said once I realized everyone was staring at me. Faine had her hands full with a counter still bursting with dirty dishes, including a cereal bowl and a couple of empty mugs, as well as taking care of Chione and her daily order for everyone at town hall. Chione was a thirty-something professional-looking human woman with medium brown skin and short, cropped black hair. She'd moved to town about a decade ago, invited by the mayor himself because she was a distant, distant descendant of his, apparently. She'd taken to life in Luna Lane like a thirsty woman to water. This morning, though, her zest for life seemed dampened. She had dark circles under her eyes, and I wondered if it was just from all the drinking last night—or from being drunk *from*. I searched for a bite mark on her neck.

"I said, you *look* better." Cable's voice drew me back to him. Right. Focus on the interloper, not the endless possibility for discovery all around us. "But *are* you?" he prodded.

"Yes, thank you." Without thinking, I sat down in front of him.

He looked taken aback.

Right. He hadn't exactly asked me to eat with him.

"How's Milton?" I asked quickly.

"Well this morning, thank you." Cable took a sip of his drink, any sudden tension in his shoulders quickly dissipating. "Doc Day stopped by, sent me off to try *the best breakfast* in town." He took a bite of his roll and his face lit up. "She wasn't kidding."

My stomach rumbled.

"You want some of mine?" he offered.

Chuckling, I waved him off. "Watch. In two minutes, Faine will bring me one of my own."

"Without even having to ask for it?"

I nodded. "Small town living."

"I was going to guess she's a mind reader, but that was my second choice," he said, wiping his sticky fingers on a napkin he'd plucked from the dispenser.

Wincing, I took a deep breath and told myself

not to panic. We didn't have mind readers in Luna Lane. That I knew of. And he was only kidding.

He picked up a pen and for the first time since sitting down with him, I zeroed in on the notepad on the table next to the stack of worn paperbacks. Desperately, my eyes scanned the scribbles, attempting to see if he was taking notes on strange citizen behaviors.

"Sorry," he said, finishing his note and putting his pen down. "I just needed to write my thought down before I lost it."

"Thought?" I snapped, rather too quickly. "About what?"

He cocked his head slightly and then clasped his hands together in his lap. He wore another dress shirt today, this one pale lavender, the upper two buttons undone. "I'm on sabbatical," he reminded me. "Sort of like a vacation, sure, but I still need to get some research done."

The tightness that had gripped my heart released in a hurry. I smoothed a lock of my hair absentmindedly, sweat prickling the back of my neck. I needed to relax. There weren't secrets waiting to be spilled around *every* corner. "What are you a professor of?" I asked, needing him not to say "mythology" or "paranormal history" or something of that nature. Did colleges even teach such things? I wouldn't know, thanks to some paranormal history of my own.

"American literature," he said.

"In Scotland?"

He shrugged. "It's not a common major or anything, but a number of literature students take the course."

The sweat dotting my body evaporated. Books, sure. Fiction. He might be creative, have an imagination. But that would be different than searching for the paranormal right under his nose.

I really needed to relax.

"Here you are," said Faine, plopping a plate with a piping hot cinnamon roll in front of me. I hadn't even noticed her finish up at the cash register. "I took a guess and picked coffee this morning," she added, placing a mug to match Cable's down beside it. "You look like you didn't get much sleep."

Smiling up at her, I inhaled the scent of java. Almost as enticing as the pastry. "You're a lifesaver," I said. "Thank you." I patted my pouch and remembered—*again*. I'd forgotten to conjure up the money.

Faine waved me off. "You have a running tab."

"Well, you really need to stop by my place later and let me pay it off." I nibbled on my roll, suddenly unable to look to see if Cable was watching me, judging me on my mooch-like behavior.

"I know you're good for it," she said. "Falcon! Get down from there!"

My attention snapped up to see what the kid had gotten himself into.

He was up on the counter, lapping up the milk

left behind in the cereal bowl Faine had yet to clean up, crouching with his knees up near his shoulders. His tongue was spraying milk everywhere.

"You know better than that!" said Faine. "Fauna, stop your brother!"

Cable leaned around Faine, and I realized she must have been blocking him from seeing what was going on. His attention diverted, I jumped up and quickly muttered under my breath, "NRUT," directing it at his chair.

With a quavering cry as if about to lose his balance, Cable spun around on his chair and he went from facing the little werewolf pup on the counter to facing the glass window overlooking the street.

Cable blinked slowly, and I decided to play along, gripping the back of his chair after the fact as if to explain how he'd spun so suddenly.

"Sorry," I said, my heart about to burst clean out of my chest. "I thought I saw a-a mouse!" I said quickly.

Falcon was on the ground now, running full tilt on all fours toward the door that led to First Taste pub. There was a hint of dark puffiness under his eyes that made him look all the more animalistic. He scratched at the wooden surface, enough to draw Cable's attention, and I had to spin him again, this time facing the front door.

"Falcon, you stay out of that bar," said Fauna. "Mama better not catch you sneaking in there again." I watched over my shoulder as she wrapped her arms around her brother's chest and heaved him away, the little boy growling and kicking and scratching at the air the whole time. I let out a deep breath as the two collapsed in a pile together near the cash register.

Cable's attention was on the ground, his legs lifted up. "There's a mouse? Where?" At least he hadn't noticed the kids' behavior.

The bell over the door jingled and in stepped Grady, a small backpack in his hand as he opened the door, a sullen Flora behind him. She wore a backpack herself and looked especially cross today.

"You *better* not have seen a rodent," shouted Faine from the kitchen.

"What's this about a rodent?" asked Grady.

"Nothing," I said quickly, my heartbeat almost too loud to hear over. "It was a mistake."

"A rodent?" Flora perked up, her nose wrinkling as she sniffed audibly.

Not *another* werewolf kid acting on her natural instincts.

"It was a napkin!" I said quickly, yanking a napkin out of the dispenser and crumpling it in my hand before throwing it to the ground.

Busted, I felt my feet practically sink into the linoleum floor as I realized Cable was staring at me, having witnessed every step of the way.

I froze, my mind no longer scrambling for solutions.

I was so, so bad at this.

"Well, thank you for your *valiant* rescue from the napkin," Cable said. "But your grip on my shoulder is getting a bit too tight." He winced.

I stared down at my left hand. I'd been gripping his *shoulder*, not the chairback. There was a suitcoat jacket on the back of the chair and I'd just assumed... I'd been too focused on everything else to see the obvious.

Yelping, I let go.

"Mouse! Mouse! Mouse!" shouted Falcon, stomping this way and that, stopping to sniff the air when he saw his big sister doing the same.

"Mouse, mouse, mouse!" Fauna joined in.

"All right, all right. You two get ready for school," Faine said to her daughters, adding to Falcon, "And you get ready for daycare."

Flora stomped her foot. "I *hate* school!"

Grady shook his head and helped Fauna into the backpack he was holding, tugging one of her beaded pigtail bands tighter.

"Hate school!" echoed Falcon.

Faine tossed a rag over her shoulder as she cleaned up the dishes her son had gotten into. "Now look what you've started. Your brother hasn't even been to school yet, and already he hates it."

"Why can't I just run around the woods all day?" Flora pouted.

Cable chuckled.

Another reason to panic. What kind of kid besides a werewolf ran around the woods all day?

"You can do that when you're older," said Faine matter-of-factly.

I winced. But Cable seemed to find it all hilarious.

Cheek kisses and hugs exchanged, Faine bid her kids goodbye for the day and Grady tipped his brown trilby hat at me before escorting the rabble out. Flora was still whining and Falcon and Fauna were singing about my non-existent mouse.

The café grew still, then quieter as they left, their muffled echoes reaching us until they'd left the block entirely.

The door to the kitchen swung loudly as Faine retreated back there. No one else was left in the café, the prime morning rush hour now over.

With the loud, grating sound of a chair pushed against a hard floor, Cable straightened himself back to his spot at the table.

"The woods, huh?" he said, lifting his coffee mug to his lips. "Despite my classroom being basically *the world*, I think I might have asked my mom something similar once."

I laughed nervously. I wondered what his mom had had to say to that—and wondered if despite them traveling all around the world, she'd kept him away from Luna Lane precisely because she hadn't wanted him involved in all of this.

He *was* Milton's family. Maybe I was over-thinking this. If he found out, his mom would stop him from blabbing, surely?

With shaky hands, I took a sip of my coffee myself.

"Before I wanted to be a professor, I wanted to be a forest ranger," he explained.

"Oh?" I managed.

"And then I wanted to be a famous investigative journalist," he added.

I choked a little. The coffee was still hot on my tongue.

His eyes twinkled for a moment before he picked up his pen and scribbled something down on his notepad. "You know, sometimes I still think I've got what it takes. I just need *one* earth-shattering story, and I'll be set."

He definitely heard me gulp at that one.

"But I never asked what you do, Dahlia. You're a fixture around here, I know that much."

"Oh, a little of this and a little of that," I mumbled, stuffing almost all of the rest of my roll in my mouth to avoid having to answer him.

"You're a freelancer?" he asked.

I nodded. That fit, right? Helping around town. He kept seeing me short on cash.

Cable stuffed his books into a folio bag he'd pulled out from under the table, then, leaning forward, he took his wallet out of his back pocket. "Does my uncle owe you for stopping by to help out?"

I shook my head quickly, chewing as hard as I could. This stuff-my-roll-in-my-mouth plan was backfiring. Cable tossed down a twenty, enough to cover both our meals and pay for a generous tip, too.

"Thank you," I mumbled through a full mouth, resigned to accept the kindness for what it was. I swallowed the last of my breakfast. "I can pay you back."

"No need." Cable moved to stand, pulling his gray suit jacket off the back of the chair and slipping it on.

Faine popped out of the kitchen just then, the loud clunk of the swinging door practically sending me sideways off my chair.

"Leaving already?" she asked, looking knowingly at me as she spoke. What? Was I supposed to stop him or something?

"Yes, it was wonderful, thank you." Cable snatched up his twenty and shuffled over to the cash register, his folio bag in hand. "I wondered if I might put in a standing order along with my uncle's for dinner, too? I haven't had dinner that good since my mom cooked for me on the regular."

Faine's eyes lit up. The best way to win her over was to compliment her cooking. "Of course!" She passed a dinner and lunch menu across the counter.

I drank the last of my coffee as my mind raced with what I was going to do. I was probably overreacting, but I didn't want to take the chance that

Luna Lane could be the big scoop Cable needed for a change in career. There had to have been some reason Ingrid had moved away—and stayed away so often. She didn't seem the type to tell her son about the paranormal and then not even bring him here firsthand to observe it. She'd homeschooled him while globetrotting, for witch's sake.

I was staring at his notepad, thinking, as the bell over the door rung again. "Thank you, Faine! Nice seeing you, Dahlia. Don't forget about tonight, you two."

"I certainly won't!" Faine called out after him.

"What's tonight?" I turned to face her.

"Games Club," she said, smiling. She was humming as she wiped down the counter.

My mind raced. Right. Today's good deed. Keeping Milton company. Wait—Faine?

"You're coming too?" I asked.

"Sure." She beamed. "He and Milton invited me last night. Grady's agreed to stay home with the kids—oh, Dahlia, we haven't done something fun like this with just grown-ups in *ages*. Motherhood has been a whirlwind."

"Oh," I said. I couldn't rightly tell her I couldn't have actually cared less about this club *now*, could I?

Besides, what was the harm? It'd give me an excuse to keep a closer eye on Cable, and I could always help out more with Milton. A cozy evening with my best friend wouldn't be so bad, either.

Yes. A nice, quiet evening with just three other people. Nothing paranormal to worry about.

Well, there was that comment Ginny had tossed out last night, but I could keep her at bay.

"I may have already told half the town," said Faine sweetly.

I was already halfway to standing, but if I hadn't been, I might have fallen out of my chair. "What? Why?"

Faine put a hand on her hip and shrugged one shoulder, sending me her best withering mom look as she pursed her lips. "Because how can you have a games *club* with just a few members?"

Sighing, I didn't even bother to ask who was going to show up tonight. I'd get there early, do my good deed before the sun set, and figure out how to turn any troublemakers away.

Blinking my eyes, I realized I'd been staring at Cable's notepad long after Cable himself had left.

"He forgot his…" I started, picking up his yellow pad.

The first few lines seemed to be notes about Emily Dickinson and James Baldwin, but there at the bottom of the page, written more hastily than the rest…

Vadas children display animal-like behavior. Strange incident with my chair.

The notepad slipped from my fingers and clattered to the floor.

Chapter Seven

I'd messed up. I didn't know how I'd ever thought I could pull the wool over his eyes—especially if no one else at all in town would help me—but I'd somehow managed to make every-thing worse.

"Excited about Games Club?"

Ginny practically made me jump out of my skin.

"What are you doing?" I hissed, looking around me. I was a block from home and Doc Day was headed my way. "Someone could see you!"

A doctor near retirement, Doc Day had white hair and had shrunk an inch or two in the time I'd known her. She wore her trademark bright floral patterns under her lab coat, a doctor's bag and stethoscope in her right hand.

"Dahlia," she said, nodding at me as she passed. Though she seemed cheerful, there were dark bags under her eyes and I wondered if she'd gotten enough rest on her trip. "Virginia."

"Good morning, Doctor Day!" said Ginny, twirling her parasol and doing a little floating curtsy at her.

Doc Day smiled and kept walking, entirely unfazed.

"Oh, no!" Ginny's voice grew high-pitched as she put a lace-covered hand atop one cheek. "Someone *did* see me! Whatever shall I do?"

"You know what I mean." I ground to a halt and put my hands on my hips to face her. One hand still clutched Cable's notepad. I'd paged through it on the walk back and hadn't found anything else to worry about, but I wasn't taking chances. I'd ripped out the incriminating page. Too bad if he lost any important research notes on it. That was what he got for snooping around town.

"I *told* you I would behave around that handsome new stranger," said Virginia. Her gaze was affixed over my head and I realized we were far too close to Milton's. He could be staring out the front window this very moment.

"Come on," I said, going to grab for her arm.

My fingers slipped right through her. She could materialize when she wanted to. She clearly didn't want to right now.

"You're in a cross mood," she said, lifting her chin in the air. "I'd prefer to spend time with you when you're more agreeable."

"*Good*," I said, my hackles rising. "Then don't come back anytime soon!"

Virginia's lips soured. "You're not being a very nice do-gooder today, Dahlia."

Do-gooder. Right. I looked up at the sun overhead —I had a number of hours to get my good deed done for the day. I just had to ask Mom something first.

I tried not to summon her too often, but sometimes... Sometimes I just didn't know what else to do.

I had no response for Virginia.

I loved Luna Lane and the people who lived here. I really did. But sometimes I wished I could just worry about *me*.

"But I can see that new stony scale is bothering you," Virginia continued, undeterred. "So I will forgive you and see you later." She made a show of turning on her heel and glided down the sidewalk.

"I didn't ask for your forgiveness!" I snapped, my stomach heavy with guilt.

I *really* needed to talk to Mom.

The moment I stepped inside my front door, Broomie's brush turned up from where she'd strewn herself in the window in the kitchen overlooking the backyard. I tossed Cable's notepad onto the end table by the door and before I could blink, she'd zoomed across the distance between us and leaped into my arms.

"Oof. Hi, sweetie," I said through a mouthful of

bristles. I patted her brush gently, careful not to get any splinters. "Getting some sunlight?" I wasn't sure why a broom needed sunlight, but she was enough like a cat that I supposed it only made sense.

As if on cue, a soft, rumbling sound echoed from her as I carried her back into the kitchen and let her nestle back on the windowsill. "You enjoy some more sun," I told her. "We're not flying today. And I need to focus—I'm calling Mom."

Broomie perked up at that.

"Yes. Mom. You can see her if I'm successful."

She rumbled and sat alert on the sill, eager not to miss her chance, no doubt. I patted her absent-mindedly as I stared out the window behind her.

My backyard was even more overgrown than my front. It wasn't just because I had no aptitude for growing plants—enchantments could easily take care of that—but that had been more of Mom's thing to begin with.

Making the backyard come to life with flowers and bushes and vegetables... That would remind me too much of her.

Besides, an unruly mess of thorns and brambles was much more in keeping with the witch lifestyle, if fairy tales were anything to go by. Though I'd only met two other witches in real life.

Right.

I had to focus.

Snatching my pointed hat off the rack by the front door, I walked over to the rune circle and inspected it for any flaws that might prove a weakness in the summoning.

All good.

My collection of completed potions beckoned me, and I nudged off the cork cap of an especially vibrant rose-colored potion.

It tasted like sewage-tainted rosewater going down, but I forced myself to swallow it and wiped my lips. I needed its power boost.

Putting the empty flask down on the shelf with a *thunk*, I approached the star drawn into the rune circle.

"RALPOP NOMANNIC, EMOC," I said, the words practically vibrating my throat. "REHTOM YM, EMOC!" I added so there'd be no mistake.

It was known to happen when the specter you were attempting to summon shared a name with a spice and a tree.

The shapes in the rune circle crackled beneath my feet, a rush of wind shooting up from the center, so strong, my hat almost blew right off my head. I gripped on to it with both hands, my voice growing louder.

"MOM, EMOC!"

The wind cut out, my hair falling limply across my face. I blew it to the side.

In the center of my circle, floating on a ghostly white broomstick of her own, was my mother.

Cinnamon Poplar. Luna Lane's only other

witch. Forever young, similar enough in appearance to me to be mistaken for my sister.

The only thing that denoted her few additional years was a stripe of white hair across one side of her head that disappeared into her bun.

And then there was the faded colors. Not as ghostly pale as Virginia, but faded everywhere, from her orange-red hair to her pointed black boots.

"Dahlia," she said, a smile lighting up her face.

"Mom!" I rushed forward, almost forgetting, for a moment—but I stopped just short of embracing her.

She'd crossed over. So, unlike Virginia, she could never be corporeal again.

Mom's posture stooped, her hand reaching toward me and curling in on itself.

The weightiness of the air between us was broken by Broomie zipping forward, spinning with a trilling sound as she flew around Mom.

Mom laughed, and I joined in, Broomie ending her little dance by touching the very tip of her brush to where Broomhannah's brush head would be. If she were able to manifest herself corporeally.

But both Mom and her companion broom were gone. These little visits were limited-time deals. Even a witch could only cross over so many times before the journey grew too difficult to make.

"You made it," I said, knowing far too well that each time could be the last.

"I did." Mom's expression grew soft. "But why

have you summoned me, darling? What's the matter?"

Suddenly struck by how foolish I'd been to waste a visit on something so trite, I grew tongue-tied, no more than a sigh escaping my lips.

"I just wanted to see you," I admitted at last. Asking her for tips on how to handle Cable seemed like such a foolish excuse.

Mom's wan cheeks glowed, but the smile quickly vanished off her face. "Is that a new scale?" She leaned in to get a closer look at my arm. "Dahlia, there are at least *seven* new scales here since I last visited."

Mortified, I tucked my left arm behind my back. "I know," I said. "I've had some slip-ups."

"You can't have *slip-ups*, honey. Each scale is larger than the last." She clucked her tongue.

"I know, but the thing is—I'm working on a way to stop the whole thing." I scrambled over to the potions book she'd left me, flipping through the pages. "There has to be something in here that can help."

"Dahlia," said Mom quietly. I could *feel* her presence hovering behind me at the edge of the rune circle. "If there were a potion that could cure your curse, don't you think I would have tried it already?"

I hadn't meant to imply she hadn't done all she could to help me.

Broomie nudged my cheek and I realized a tear was slipping out from between my eyelashes.

"I know you did everything you could," I said. "But you couldn't have thought to try *every* potion in here."

"*Every* potion?"

"Well, every potion I *can*. Some need ingredients I can't get in and around town. Or are too difficult to procure." There were at least a few that required vampire venom, and I just wasn't in the right frame of mind to ask the vampires for a favor. I sighed and shut the book. A cloud of dust escaped from between the endlessly dusty pages.

"Some of the potions in that book... They could get dangerous."

"I know." Turning back around to face Mom, I leaned against the table. "I'll be careful."

Mom's voice was stern. "Dahlia, focus on the good deeds. Not a miracle potion cure."

"I'm a *witch*, Mom. There has to be *something*—"

"*Dahlia.*"

I chewed my lip but said nothing.

Mom's head cocked and she floated swiftly around the perimeter of the circle. "What's that I sense...?"

Whatever she was talking about was news to me, too.

"What?" I asked, suddenly alert, my hand clenched at my side and at the ready.

"Eithne," said Mom quietly. "Her dark magic... It's faint, but it's here. In town."

"*What?*" I hadn't even picked up on that. "What do you mean?"

Mom tapped a finger to her lips. "I wish I knew. When was I here last?"

I thought it over. I'd summoned her late last year, on her birthday. "It's been six months." *A long, lonely six months*, a small part of me thought. But that hadn't been true. I'd had Faine and Ginny and Goldie and Arjun and Milton, even if they'd all had their own things to do. And Leana…

"Leana passed away," I said. Mom might have seen her on the other side, so she probably knew.

Mom looked dazed for a second, her eyes widening. "When?"

"When?" I asked, puzzled. I supposed one lost track of time in the realm beyond. "About three months ago."

"No," Mom said quietly, more to herself than me. She slid off Broomhannah and paced the circumference of the circle, her broom trailing behind her like a loyal puppy dog. "No, no." She stopped and looked straight at me. "What else have I missed?"

I jolted back, her panic palpable. "Nothing. Uh…" I thought back. "Jeremiah's favorite cow had another calf. Mayor Abdel ran unopposed and won reelection again. Faine's middle daughter started school… Oh, and Milton's nephew came to town yesterday. He's here for a few months."

"Cable?" Mom asked.

How did *she* know him? Well, she'd probably paid better attention to Leana and Milton talking about him than I had.

"Yes," I said. "He's actually why I thought to summon you. No one's being careful enough around him, Mom. I'm afraid he'll figure out Luna Lane's secret and then…" And then what? Reporters and tourists would descend upon the town? The government would quarantine us all and experiment on us like rats?

Maybe everyone else could escape in time to avoid either scenario.

But me? I only had one place I could call home.

Mom waved her hand in the air. "Don't you worry about Cable and Luna Lane's secrets. Ingrid is good people. If she didn't tell him, it was for a reason, but she wouldn't let him blab if he does find out."

She had a point there.

"But the rest…" Mom tapped her forefinger over her lips. "Was the cow infertile?"

"Huh?" I thought over what she'd asked. "The one that gave birth? Not that I know of."

"Hmm." Mom kept pacing, but she stopped, her hand growing even fainter in front of her. Broomhannah's shaft was fading in a similar way.

"We have to go, darling," she said, rushing over. "So listen to what I have to say. Leana didn't cross over."

I cocked my head. "How can you be sure? Maybe you just didn't cross paths—"

"*Listen*," said Mom, cutting me off. Half her arms were gone now. "I know because I am aware of every life that passes over from Luna Lane. I wouldn't have missed Leana. Poor Milton." Her voice broke a little, but she straightened, clearly with plenty more to say. "That means she didn't die. Not normally."

"I went to her funeral," I pointed out. "Open casket," I felt obliged to add.

Mom shook her head. She was like a floating torso now, Broomhannah mostly just her brush. Broomie cooed sadly beside me.

"Something is afoul with her death," Mom said resolutely. "You have to investigate. With the stench of Eithne's magic coming from town, I fear the worst."

"Worse than death?" I asked, not thinking. I was talking to a dead woman right now, and she seemed to be doing all right, considering.

Mom's expression went grim. "I'm afraid so, Dahlia. I fear she may have been murdered—and not in any conventional way."

But before I could ask more, the last of my mother disappeared, the glow of the rune circle flickering out to nothing.

Chapter Eight

*L*eana may have been murdered. Her soul wasn't resting in peace in the realm beyond —it wasn't even living it up in town as a specter with unfinished business like Virginia.

And there were traces of Eithne, the witch who'd cursed me—who'd been responsible for my mother's death—having used her dark magic in town.

And all of this had passed me by completely.

Roaring in anger, I picked up my potions book, ripped open a nearby cupboard, and shoved it inside, slamming the door shut.

My heart thumped wildly inside my chest.

No more worrying about myself and breaking this vexing curse on me. No more stressing so much about Cable and keeping Luna Lane a secret from the rest of the world.

Not until I figured out what that evil witch was up to, and what in the world had happened to poor Leana.

Broomie let out a distressed little yip and came over to nudge her brush against me.

I hugged her and cried a little into her bristles, allowing myself just a few minutes more of self-pity.

All right. I checked the hour. Plenty of time before the sun set. I could pop out a quick inconsequential good deed and get focusing on the real problem.

"Stay here," I told Broomhilde. Her brush sagged.

"I'm going over to Milton's," I explained. "Cable's there." I stepped over to the front window in my living room and peeked outside. "If you're careful, you can go across the street and ask Goldie or Arjun for some more cornhusks, okay?"

She wagged her handle happily.

Opening the front door, I stopped, realizing I still had my pointed hat on. It'd help me with any magic I had to perform, especially since I'd blown through any boost the rosewood potion had offered me by summoning a witch from the dead.

But Cable...

Sighing, I hung up the hat and grabbed his notepad from the end table beside it.

I didn't lock the door behind me as I descended down the bramble-covered walkway. There were only two people I particularly cared to keep out of my house. A lock wouldn't stop a determined amateur investigative journalist—and it wouldn't be necessary if he was just an innocent professor on sabbatical. And no amount of locks or magic could stop Eithne.

Thanks to the town pitching in, Milton's yard was much tidier than mine. The roses Leana had taken such great care of were still neatly trimmed in the hedges around the front and side of the house. I could have used magic to make them neat and tidy, but yardwork often counted as my good deed, and that meant I'd have to put my back in it a little.

I wiped my forehead with my forearm, the sweat accumulating there at the thought of the task ahead of me getting impossible to ignore.

Milton never locked his door, either, but I rang the doorbell.

Cable appeared a moment later, the corner of his lip twerked up into a smile.

"Ah. You found it," he said by way of greeting.

I stared blankly at him.

Oh. Right. I held the notepad out to him. "You left it at the café."

"Thanks." He flipped through the pages and came to that last page I'd torn out. He stared up at me. I said nothing, and he just smirked.

"Do you want to come in?" he asked instead of prodding me about the missing page.

"Yes, thank you." Taking a deep breath, I stepped inside. Cable put his notepad down on an end table next to his folio bag and a stack of worn paperbacks. "Sorry for the mess," he said, and my do-gooder instinct perked up. Only I looked around, and there wasn't any mess to clean at all, unless he counted those books in slight disarray.

"Uncle Milton!" Cable called out down the hall. "Dahlia from next door is here!"

"Virginia?" Milton called out.

Cable chuckled. "He really likes this Virginia. Goldie told me she's a little eccentric. I hope I get to meet her."

I put a palm to my face. Why hadn't Goldie just told him Virginia was someone from Milton's youth or something?

"She's... uh... Um, are there any little odd jobs Milton needs done?" I asked as I followed him to where Milton was sitting in his room. His TV was on, but he had his back to it, his armchair shifted to face the green gaming table, a folding chair brought out across from it. There were two sheets of paper, pens, and a cup on the table, five dice scattered across its surface.

"Oh, no, don't worry about it. You're our guest." He paused as Milton looked up. "We're playing Yatzy," Cable explained.

"*Yatzy*, like...?"

Cable shrugged. "Uncle Milton seemed to have

saved a few bucks by investing in knock-off versions of the big games."

"Yatzy!" said Milton, jabbing a gnarled finger at the dice.

Cable leaned over the table to inspect the dice. "Hmm, so it is," he said, his eyes twinkling. "But Milton, you had your three rolls. Did you change this four to a five while I went to get the door?"

Milton scratched his chin. A wisp of a beard had begun growing in. "I rolled Yatzy," he said after a bit.

"All right," said Cable, amused. "Then record it on your sheet." He turned back to me. "Can I offer you something? We just had lunch, but—"

"Oh, Milton! Don't do that! I *hate* cheating! You know you turned that die when he wasn't looking."

Cable whirled around just as my jaw hit the floor.

Virginia stood behind Milton—*stood*, at least, instead of floated—pointing to Milton's score sheet.

He muttered something incomprehensible and waved a dismissive hand at her, writing down his score anyway.

"Come on now!" Virginia put her hands on her hips. "You are a lot of things, Milton, but you were never a cheater." She was still most definitely in her cream-and-white turn-of-the-twentieth-century attire, and her skin was too white to truly be believed, but she seemed to have dulled her eerie glow for the most part. I hadn't known she could do that. "What would Leana think?" she added.

That seemed to get through to him. He put the pen down and peered around the room. "Leana?" he said softly. "Leana, did you bring the game back down?"

Cable cleared his throat and made his way over to Virginia. "I don't believe we've been introduced," he said, extending a hand. "Cable Woodward, Milton's nephew."

"Virginia Kincaid," said Ginny. I stared and stared at her hand as she hesitated to take Cable's. But she did, and the hands touched, connecting. Cable's shiver at the feel of her cold skin even through her lace glove was obvious from here.

"So *you're* the infamous Virginia."

Ginny seemed flattered. "One and the same." She fluffed at her perfectly coiffed hair. "You can call me 'Ginny,' Mr. Woodward."

"Then please, call me 'Cable.'"

Virginia's wan eyes lit up. "Ooo. Don't mind if I do, Mr. Cable."

Cable chuckled and gestured to the folding chair. "Would you like to finish my score card?"

Virginia went to take the seat. "Why, thank you."

For how surprisingly well this aggravating set of circumstances was going, I wouldn't have expected my throat to be constricting so tightly, my breathing to become so ragged. My mouth flopped open like a fish's because I had no idea what to say.

"I didn't see you come in," said Cable quietly. He'd shuffled out to the hallway and appeared back with that darn notepad in his hands, along with a pencil.

Bananaberries.

"I… I let her in," I said, jumping between Virginia and Cable. Virginia wasn't at all concerned, instead gathering the dice up and putting them in the cup.

"Nonsense," said Virginia as she shook the dice. "Milton lets me come and go as I please." She rolled the dice and let out a little squeal. "Oh! One roll and a full house!"

I glared daggers at the back of her head. She wasn't supposed to be here in front of Cable, and she *definitely* wasn't supposed to make covering her tracks all that much harder.

The scratch of a pencil on paper drew my attention back to Cable. He watched Virginia as his uncle took his turn.

"Small straight," Milton said.

"No, Milton," said Virginia, her voice clipped. "You have two twos and two threes. You need two, three, four, and five for that. Roll again." She fussed with the dice for him, putting some back into the cup.

"Small straight!" Milton crossed his arms.

Virginia huffed. "Now, Milton, I know things

aren't always clear for you these days, but you know I *hate* and I do mean *hate* cheaters! Now *roll again*." She slammed the cup in front of him.

"Virginia," I said quickly, already sensing Milton's anxiety rise. I put my hand over the cup. "It's fine, Milton. Write down your small straight."

He picked up his pen.

"Dahlia Poplar," said Virginia, aghast, "I never took you for a helper of *cheaters*!"

That reminded me. Helper.

"I really need to do something to help out," I said quickly, my mouth snapping shut when Cable tapped the eraser of his pencil to his lips. "Virginia. Please."

Virginia jerked down the cuff of her sleeve, smoothing out imagined wrinkles with great fastidiousness. "I imagine you do," she said. "But I don't know *how* we can have a Games Club if we're going to ignore rampant cheating."

"Abraham's a cheater," spat Milton. He actually spat onto the ground beside the table. "Thinks because his wife is drunk, too, he can get away with anything."

Drunk? Had the Davises been known to get a little tipsy on Saturday nights?

"Well, you're a cheater, too," said Virginia, crossing her legs tightly. "And I don't see the point in playing with cheaters."

"Virginia, if you're not here to help ease

Milton's anxieties, I don't think you get the point of Games Club," I said.

"Nonsense. Milton invited me, and then Faine did—this is supposed to be a legitimate town activity."

I rolled my eyes as Milton picked up the cup and began shaking the dice within it. This time he rolled a three and a four. "Small straight," he said, firmer this time, the two and five already on the table.

"Small straight indeed." Virginia beamed and sat straighter in her chair.

Cable watched it all with far too much fascination, scribbling something more on his notepad.

Argh! I didn't have time to be worried about this.

"Leana?" Milton asked, reaching up to tap my arm. "Did you bring the game back down?"

"It's Dahlia," I said softly. Leana and I looked nothing alike. Judging by the wedding photo on his bedside table, we never had. "What game? Evidence?"

That was what he'd asked me to go get the day before, though he'd known it had been me he'd been asking.

Milton nodded, his lips hardening into a grim line as Virginia took her turn, celebrating again on her third roll. "Evidence," he said softly. "Leana, be careful," he added. "Don't..." He let out a sharp cry.

Cable tossed aside his notepad and joined me at his uncle's side. "Milton, what's wrong?"

Milton started sobbing. Even Virginia went whiter, if that were possible, the dice dropping with several clunks from her hand to the cup.

"Leana played the game," Milton said, wiping one eye with the back of his hand. He sniffled deeply, the snot dripping out of his nose. He seemed the most lucid he'd been in ages. "She played the game. We played it wrong. And then she died."

Chapter Nine

"A game didn't kill Aunt Leana," said Cable soothingly. He wrapped an arm around him and gripped him by the elbow. "It's okay. Why don't we go to the restroom and get cleaned up? Okay, Uncle Milton?"

"She was right. We have to play. We just played it wrong. Wrong winner." Milton was mumbling now. Standing with his nephew's help, Milton tapped the younger man's arm. "Cable?" he asked.

"That's right, Uncle." Cable patted his uncle's shoulder. "You remember me?"

"You're so big." Milton studied the man so much taller than him with awe.

"You say that every time you see me," teased Cable as the two wandered down the hall. "Maybe you're just small."

Milton seemed to find that a riot, his laughter echoing out even through the closed door.

I whirled on Virginia.

She lifted her hands in surrender. "Don't you start, Miss Poplar. I was *invited* to this Games Club."

"Games Club isn't until tonight, apparently." I quickly shook my head to clear it. "And that's hardly the problem with you showing up—but never mind that." I took hold of her wrist, found it solid, and yanked her up. "Come with me."

"But where are we going?" she asked, stumbling, clearly wobbly on two feet. Sure enough, she started floating behind me.

"NEPO," I said to the latch on the gate leading upstairs before tiptoeing up the steps, dragging Virginia behind me.

When we reached the top, my fist closed in on itself, Virginia's pale, ghastly glow lighting up the dim upstairs hallway as she made herself incorporeal.

"Miss Poplar, you explain yourself right now." She cradled her wrist to her chest as if I'd hurt her.

A hot breath escaped between my lips. Virginia was not my first choice of confidant when it came to what my mom had told me, but she would have to do. "My mom told me Leana was murdered. Possibly by Eithne." She hadn't said that part, but what else would explain the presence of dark magic in town?

Virginia blinked rapidly as she floated a few inches off the ground so our eyes met. "What are you telling me? You spoke to your *mother*?"

I twirled a lock of hair around my finger. "I summon her every so often," I admitted.

"But she passed…" Virginia bit her lip. "You know you can only summon her so many times, right?"

"Yes." I tapped a foot. "That's not the issue here. Mom sensed Eithne's magic in town. And she told me Leana never crossed."

Ginny frowned. "She's not still here. I would have definitely noticed another lingering specter."

"That's what I thought." Tugging on my dress skirt to steady myself, I turned and looked up at the attic hatch above us. "She collapsed in the attic, didn't she?" I hadn't been there, but I remembered. Doc Day had swung by to check on Milton. She hadn't been able to find Leana. Milton had kept saying, "She went upstairs. She went to bring it back down."

I'd never bothered to wonder what "it" had been before now.

Doc Day had found the attic ladder down, had climbed up and found Leana dead in the attic. Heart attack, she'd suspected. Sudden, without warning, but not unheard of at Leana's age, with the stress of caring for a spouse with dementia, with the exertion of climbing up the ladder, perhaps.

Jeremiah, Mayor Abdel, and a number of the stronger men in town had helped bring Leana down. Even Draven had offered to help as soon as the sun had set. Milton had had to invite him in for that.

I'd watched them by Milton's side in his living-room-turned-bedroom, holding his hand as the men had carried her down, a sheet over her, taking her out to the hearse for transport to the local funeral parlor.

Draven's red-rimmed steel gray eyes had looked glossy as he'd stood on the porch, watching the hearse drive away. He hadn't even bothered to look at me the whole time he'd been in the house, not that I'd much cared at that moment.

I remembered Qarinah, her beautiful face drained, as she tried to comfort him with a sideways embrace. Ravana had offered the same and Draven had pushed the women away, turning into a bat and flapping off into the night.

Sheriff Roan had done his best to explain to Milton and spent the night at his side.

"Go home and rest now, Lia," he'd told me. "We're all the town's do-gooders now." He'd meant that we'd all chip in toward Milton's care so he wouldn't have to be sent away. Just as the town had with Mrs. Flores when I'd been a kid.

Roan had never ordered an autopsy. There wouldn't have been a need in Luna Lane.

Not if that vile evil witch was nowhere to be found.

"You want me to go up there?" Virginia asked, pointing to the attic hatch. Her voice cracked, but she nodded, as much to herself as anything, and flew right up and through the ceiling.

A small drip of her ectoplasm hit my nose.

"You could have waited for me to open the hatch," I muttered, wiping the goo away. "NEPO," I said softly, pointing up at the door.

The hatch popped open and the ladder slid down.

Rustles echoed out from the dark attic above as I ascended, the bit of light trickling in through the high-up window doing little to help me see anything other than the particles of dust that flew up in the air.

A shadow darted out from beside me, a shrieking little squeak making me cry out as I jumped and stubbed my toe—hard—on something as solid as a rock.

I forced deep breaths out through my lips as I shook my foot in the air. "WOLG," I said, holding my hand aloft. My fingertips emitted a soft, orange glow upon a dusty bowling ball on the floor.

"Well, that's a hazard," I said, bending to pick it up by the finger holes. Some of the dust shifted away, revealing the ball to be a bright red color.

We didn't even have a bowling lane in Luna Lane. Not currently anyway. There was a shuttered one downtown, but that had closed decades ago.

But if any human in town remembered going to it, it would have been Milton. He was our oldest human resident left, now that Leana was gone.

Hobbling on my sore toe, I slid the heavy ball on the bottom shelf of a nearby shelving unit packed with a lifetime of memories.

A furry, twitching set of whiskers popped out at me from behind the ball just as my hand slipped out, something crusty catching on my fingertips.

I shrieked, surprised more than anything, and fell flat on my rear end.

"It's just a mouse," said Virginia from wherever she'd been. She floated past me, leaving the air she touched so cold, it took me several seconds to stop shivering.

"I know," I said, nodding to the fuzzy little creature and wiping off the grime on my dress. I wondered if it was the same one who'd unintentionally shown me where the Evidence game had been stashed.

Evidence. Could that have possibly been what Leana had come up here for the day she'd died?

Milton had told me as much. He'd sent her to go find it. She'd been going to "bring it back down." I just hadn't put two and two together.

"Ginny, can you check that shelf?" I asked, pointing to the very top of the shelving unit across the attic, where I'd found the game.

Virginia floated over to it, hovering, poking her head into the very small space between the top of the shelf and the ceiling. "What am I—Oh!"

"Oh?" I asked, scrambling back to my feet. Out

of habit, I grabbed for the rickety stepstool and realized this wasn't part of my good deed, so pish posh, I could use a little magic. "ETATIVEL." I pointed to my feet and soared up beside Virginia, her ghastly glow and my illuminated fingertips bringing light to a dark corner that never otherwise saw it.

It was the first time I'd actually gotten a look at where the game had been since my head had never gotten this high the first time.

It was dirty. Dust and cobwebs were so thick, you could peel them off the wood. Little, elongated brown bits made it clear my mouse friend had a favorite location to relieve himself back behind where the game had been. There might have even been bits of black mold far back in the corner. That could be dangerous.

"NAELC," I said, waving my fingers. The mold, the droppings, the dust and all glowed and then went away.

Leaving behind an excess of pale red slime that looked familiar somehow, but I'd never seen—

"Ectoplasm," said Virginia. She twirled in place, as if checking her derriere for stains. "But definitely not mine. Mine's green."

"Red ectoplasm?" I asked aloud. And my enchantment hadn't cleaned it away.

Hesitatingly, I reached out my illuminated hand and skimmed the surface. I cried out, pulling back my fingers, which immediately lost their glow. It had *burned* to the touch. Not like Virginia's ectoplasm at all.

There was a tingling in my chest, and my legs grew shaky, despite the fact that I was standing on nothing but air.

I had to get a sample.

Popping an empty vial out of my pouch, I scooped up the goo inside, muttering, "LOOC," over and over to keep my fingertips cool. It didn't really seem to work. Corking the small vial and tucking it in the elastic on my belt, I let out a cry as my levitation magic broke and I fell to the ground.

"Ouch, ouch, ouch." I rubbed my bruised tailbone.

"Oh! Look!" Virginia showed no concern for my fall, instead hovering by the little skylight and looking outdoors.

I was about to snap at her when I heard the muffled sound of Cable's voice, shouting out Milton's name.

"What's happening?" I asked, jumping to my feet. "ETATIVEL," I said again.

My feet didn't move.

I stared down at the red goo in my vial.

Eithne's magic?

Was this what my mom had sensed? No wonder. It was so nearby. My house was right there. That window overlooked my backyard.

"Milton has a shovel," Virginia explained. She somehow looked paler—no, *fainter* was probably the better word. Perhaps it was a trick of the light. "And he's just climbed the fence and landed in that mess of brambles you call a garden."

"*What?*"

Despite the fact that I was now investigating a magical murder, that my own magic was muted in the presence of this foul substance, Virginia couldn't have told me anything that would have surprised me more just then if she'd tried.

Chapter Ten

*S*crambling down the attic ladder and then the stairs, I ran outside, ignoring Virginia's commentary, though suddenly remembering the fact that a *ghost* was trailing behind me, I swirled on her as we reached the overgrowth at the side of my house.

"Ground," I said, pointing to her feet. "Glow."

She rolled her eyes and lowered herself, patting her perfectly coifed hair. "Yes, yes." Her glow faded and her paleness managed to just barely seem plausible. But there was still something… *off* about her.

"Are you fading?" I asked.

She gasped, a hand on her chest. "Are you joshing me? I'm as pale as a gentile lady has any right to be." She produced her parasol out of thin air. The canopy was made of cream-colored lace and she often boasted that the handle and ferrule on top were made of solid porcelain. "Why, I'm no whiter than the porcelain ferrule on this very dainty sunshade."

There she went, bragging again. As if any of that mattered now that it was all spectral nothingness. "Never mind."

"Now can you explain to me how this red ectoplasm has anything to do with Leana's death?"

I snapped my mouth closed. I didn't know if it had anything to do with it. "I'm more worried about Milton right now."

"All right, all right." Virginia's voice echoed from behind me. "Just checking. I'm not sure I'm entirely following."

I *really* needed to get Faine or Goldie or someone else to help me with this.

Or Sheriff Roan. Duh.

But first things first.

"Milton, please." The crunching of brush and brambles beneath Cable's feet from up ahead pulled me in the right direction. "This is dangerous. You might have hurt yourself already."

Pulling at a vine dangling overhead, I muttered, "EVOM," to it, but nothing happened.

Right. The evil ectoplasm.

I tugged on the vine instead until it gave way. "*Milton!*"

There was a *thunk* and a *whap*. Sounds I couldn't quite place until Virginia spoke up.

"That must be why he had the shovel."

So he was *digging* in my backyard?

"Leave me be!" roared Milton.

With one more push of a bramble, I found them, toward the very back, almost up against the fence.

"What's going on?" I asked.

Cable jumped and spun around. He looked as if he'd seen a ghost.

Though not the one behind me. He'd already seen her and hadn't seemed alarmed in the least.

"I don't know what came over him," Cable explained as Milton tossed a small amount of dirt over the fence. "I was helping him wash his face in the bathroom when he shouted his wife's name and ran outside to his garden shed. He grabbed the shovel and before I could get him to hand it back, he sprinted around me and hopped the fence!" Cable wiped his brow, leaving behind a small streak of dirt, which only accentuated his rugged good looks. "He's surprisingly spry when he wants to be. I don't even…" He looked around. "Is this your property, Dahlia?"

"Yes." My neck and ears grew impossibly warm. "I might have let my garden go the past decade or so."

Cable chewed his lip but turned back to his uncle.

"Oh!" cried Virginia as Milton tossed another pile of dirt. She'd produced a ghostly handkerchief from thin air and covered her nose with it, as if scents were still an issue for her.

"Milton," I said softly, stepping around Cable on unsteady feet. My ballet slipper caught on a root sticking up from underground and I fell against the visiting professor.

"Sorry. Thank you," I said sheepishly, our lips so close as I looked up, I nearly jumped backward out of my skin.

"Oh, my," said Virginia. Her handkerchief had morphed into a paper fan, which she unfolded and used to fan herself.

Thank the skies Cable wasn't looking at her.

In fact, he was just staring straight at me.

Swallowing, I got back to the more important matter at hand. "Milton, please hand me the shovel."

"No." He grunted and dug the shovel in deeper, hitting something hard with a clang. He nearly tumbled, but Cable stepped up to steady him.

"Milton, ask me to do it," I said.

Cable rubbed the back of his head but quickly seemed to decide I was tricking the old man into relinquishing the shovel. He stepped back and gestured at me, as if to say, *"Have a go."*

"Dahlia?" asked Milton, studying me up and down.

"Yes, Milton. It's Dahlia. Please ask me to help you."

If he was at all lucid, he'd know I needed it.

Milton's gaze traveled behind me to the afternoon sky, probably wondering if I was in a hurry or if I'd have time to complete the task he assigned to me.

"Please help me, Dahlia." He handed me the shovel with both hands, reverently. "Dig them up. Still the torment of my heart."

I took it from him, feeling a patch on my left arm tingle with the movement. The acceptance of the good deed for the day.

The most somber and ominous-sounding good deed I'd ever undertaken.

"Here?" I asked, digging the tip of the shovel into the dirt.

Milton nodded. "Behind your mother's garden, behind the bushes. As far back as we could bury them."

I dug in.

"Dahlia, you don't have to actually—" started Cable.

At the same time, Virginia said, "Well, if *that* isn't the most eerie request I've ever heard."

I was already on my second stroke. Digging as deep as I could, shifting around the hard rock the shovel scraped up against, tossing the dirt over the fence and into Milton's backyard as he'd been doing.

"Milton, let's get inside," Cable offered.

"No." The old man actually dug his heel into the dirt. "I stay until she finds them."

Virginia laughed nervously. "What are we talking about here, dear old Milton? Buried jewels?

Time capsules? I buried a few of those myself in my short time on—"

I clanged the shovel extra hard against the fence, which elicited a yip from Virginia. She went quiet.

"Dahlia, you don't have to humor him this much," said Cable softly, reaching for the shovel.

I yanked it out of his reach and stared at him, narrowing my brows. "Let me do this for him."

Cable's troubled expression didn't lift, but he stepped back.

I kept digging.

Virginia kept babbling. With the strain of the effort, I was having trouble even properly seeing her. She almost seemed translucent again anytime I looked over at her.

Milton groaned with every bit of progress I made.

No one left. No one helped me. I had to do this all by myself.

Half an hour into it, Cable left briefly and when he returned, he handed glasses of water out to all of us. Virginia cradled hers awkwardly, Milton fluffed his away, and I gulped mine down in three long, glorious sips.

"I can take over," said Cable.

I shook my head and handed him the glass without a word.

I never stopped to think about what I'd find—if anything, if Milton was lucid enough not to have imagined whatever he was looking for in the first place. There was just the work, the heavy jostling of the little flask of ectoplasm against my hip. Even if I couldn't use magic right now regardless, I regretted not dropping off the foul stuff inside. It seemed to burn hotter at my hip with every inch of progress made.

At last, I didn't know how much later, I struck something hard. It didn't sound like rock.

Working to uncover the find, I pushed away the surrounding dirt.

And revealed the pointing finger of a skeletal hand.

Milton let out a gargled cry and collapsed to his knees, Cable slowing the fall.

The tingling on my forearm vanished, my good deed for the day complete.

I sat on the front porch of my house, watching as "the city boys and girls" carted away the skeletal remains of two adult human bodies buried deep in the farthest reaches of my backyard. The sun was nearly set, the last rays of twilight only just enough to see by before the streetlights would turn on to wash it all out with an artificial glare.

Virginia rocked herself steadily on my log rocking chair, mumbling prayers. She was so washed out, it was like she'd seen a ghost. Still, she somehow seemed more solid than she had earlier. That was a relief.

Next door, Sheriff Roan spoke with Cable on Milton's front porch, the professor gesticulating animatedly and consistently running a hand through his dark hair. He'd taken his glasses off at some point, so he must not have needed them at all times.

"What's that on your dress?" Virginia asked, her mumbling finally becoming coherent.

That was the first question she had for me?

I looked down. I was splattered with dirt. I scraped away at some of it. There was a streak of gray-rust-colored grime that didn't match the rest of it that was especially stubborn to scrape away with my nails.

I peeked to make sure Cable wasn't looking my way, then scooched to turn my back to him for good measure. "NAELC." I pointed my hands at the dress and it all went away, the fabric and my hands and arms as clean as they'd been this morning.

Even the simple movement sent an ache up my arm. I rubbed over the "tattoo." There was an enchantment for sore muscles, but right now… I was almost too tired to utter it.

Virginia nodded thoughtfully and chewed her lip. After a minute, she asked, "Do you think Milton killed them?"

"I don't know," I said honestly. "But I can't picture that."

"Who are they?" she asked. Her brow furrowed. "One couldn't be Leana—"

"Too decomposed. Besides, we saw her get buried."

"But her soul didn't cross over." Virginia clucked her tongue. "And what of those two poor souls?"

"We have to know who they were first."

I strode inside, telling Virginia to let me know if Roan wanted anything else from me. I hadn't let the officials from the coroner's office inside, and I could feel their glares burning my back for the rough terrain they'd had to traverse through to get the bodies out of the ground. I could have enchanted the overgrowth away before they'd arrived, but that would have been hard to explain to Cable.

If they had a warrant, I'd make sure everything... odd... was out of sight. But for now, this was Roan's jurisdiction, and he knew I'd had nothing to do with those deaths, whoever they had been.

Broomie soared over from her pet bed before the fireplace, sliding her shaft beneath my rear and lifting me up for a quick, short float around the room.

"Whoa, whoa, girl." I patted her brush. She lowered me gently in front of the table where I'd stuck the red ectoplasm.

I didn't know how Milton had known those skeletons had been out there—he wouldn't explain, he'd just started mumbling his wife's name—and I couldn't even begin to guess who they were. They'd been out there a long time, clearly, but no one from town was missing. There was no enchantment that I knew of that could tell me the answer, and besides, the county coroner could tell us more in a matter of days. Faster if he made good on a favor he apparently owed Roan.

I *did* know something wasn't right about Leana's death, and this ectoplasm, this was something I might be able to work with.

I flipped through the potions book, searching for anything to do with ghosts and spectral discharges. I'd settled on maybe just putting it in the rune circle and chanting an enchantment for it to seek its source when there was a knock on the front door.

Virginia popped through the wall, squishing her own green ectoplasm down the knots in the wood. I really wished she'd stop doing that.

"It's Faine," she said. "And Ravana—and Draven." She shook both her forearms tightly in front of her chest, like it was the best news she'd heard all day.

Faine made sense. But Ravana—and *Draven?*

They knocked on the door again.

Straightening my dress, I grabbed my pointed hat off the stand and slapped it on before opening the door.

"Hello, Faine!" said Virginia brightly.

"Hello, Ginny," Faine said amiably to the ghost somewhere behind me. Then she turned to me, dropping a couple of big bags to the floor and launching herself into my arms. "Oh my goodness. I can't believe what we heard—two dead bodies! In *your* backyard!"

I hugged her back, though eventually I had to tap her shoulder and point out she was squeezing out my last breath.

"Sorry," she said, tucking her dark hair behind her ear.

"It's okay." I smiled at her. "I appreciate you coming."

"We didn't really come to console you over buried dead bodies," said a smooth, silky voice. Ravana. "They've been out there how long and no one cared until today? Boohoo." Wow, talk about empathy. "Faine convinced us to join Games Club. It sounds *delightful.*"

I glanced over Faine's shoulder at Ravana and Draven, both still on the porch and glaring icily my way.

Games Club? *Them?*

They just stood there, the both of them.

"Oh," I scrambled to say. "You may both come inside."

They did, the requisite permission granted to vampires entering an abode on private property, and I shut the door behind them.

Draven had had permission to come and go as he pleased years before. I hadn't realized that could ever wear off. Perhaps it changed with the mood of the house owner.

Or maybe he was just being polite. To me or to Ravana, whom I supposed I'd never had an opportunity to invite inside.

But Draven? Being polite?

"Hello." Virginia folded her hands over her waist.

Neither vampire acknowledged her.

Virginia huffed, and hands on her hips, floated back silently.

Draven strutted around the house like he'd been asked to become king of the castle. His condescending sneer was more than a little aggravating when he ran a pale digit over the surface of my potions table and came back with a bit of dust he flicked off his finger.

As if I owed *him* a clean house. I never would have imagined he'd set foot in it again.

"Dahlia?" Faine's voice snapped me back to the conversation she'd apparently been having with me.

"I love what you've done with the place." Ravana, her hands on her hips as she sashayed about the den Mom had made our rune circle room, sounded anything but genuine.

"How's Milton doing?" Faine asked, ignoring the vampires' unasked-for house inspection.

"I'll go check!" said Virginia, flying back through the wall instead of opening the door.

Both vampires' heads turned to the ectoplasm dripping down the wall.

"What is up with her?" Ravana asked, her nose wrinkling in disgust.

"She did seem awfully pale," added Draven. So I wasn't the only one who'd thought so. Only I'd thought her color had been improving. I rubbed my eyes. Then again, it wasn't like I'd stared at her in a while. I was so tired, and my muscles still ached. Draven turned away from the dirtied wall. "Though her ectoplasm remains as bright as day."

"NAELC," I said, but nothing happened. Sighing, I walked closer to the door, as far away from the vile red ectoplasm on my table as I could manage. "NAELC," I tried again, and the green goo disappeared. What was it about the red version that made it so resistant?

"Now do the rest of the house," suggested Ravana, an eyebrow arched.

"Ravana," whispered Draven under his breath. He nudged her and she shrugged.

"Did you leave Qarinah all by herself to run the pub tonight?" I snapped. Under my breath, I muttered, "YDIT" to the table Draven had found dust on.

"She asked some of the day shift if they wanted extra hours," said Ravana.

"Todd and Jamie," added Draven. He pointed a sharp look at the vampire who'd sired him. "Surely, they've worked for us long enough that you know their names by now."

She flung her dark hair over her shoulder. "Bloodbag 1 and Bloodbag 2," she joked. No one else found it amusing.

Just then, a divine scent wafted toward me from the bags Faine had brought in with her, my stomach rumbling.

She caught me staring. "I brought enough for everyone. For the whole club." She said the last part haltingly, with reverence, giving the loss of the evening's plans enough weight, it was like she'd lost a puppy.

"I doubt you packed anything for Draven and me in *that*," quipped Ravana.

I gave her a death stare. She gave it right back.

Virginia popped right through my wall, followed by the gushy sound of a new veil of ectoplasm dripping down. I did hope she'd remembered to *knock* on Milton's door rather than fly through it. "Milton's in a state," she said. She did look rather faint again. What was up with her today? Perhaps appearing as human as she could, manifesting herself physically, was wearing on her. "Cable isn't sure what to do. Milton keeps saying, 'Games Club, Games Club.' When I told Milton Luna Lane's next generation of the club was all gathered here, Cable asked if we might come over despite everything that's happened." She looked pleased.

I exchanged a look with Faine, then with

Draven, who shrugged. "Dead bodies don't tend to rattle me."

Ravana laughed. "I'd hate to think we wasted a trip."

I really wanted to study the red ectoplasm, but... Milton needed us. Cable needed us. And there was plenty more to uncover yet. How had Milton known about the bodies buried in my backyard?

What, if anything, did they have to do with Leana's death?

"Okay," I said. "But before we go... The rest of you should know—"

Draven interrupted. "Don't let your new boyfriend figure out we're paranormal." He hooked his thumbs in the belt loops at his waist, thrusting his pelvis forward.

"Not my boyfriend, and yes, but that's not what I wanted to say." Irritation bubbled up inside me, but I took a deep breath and shoved it down. "I summoned my mother—and she told me that Leana never crossed over."

The room grew quiet. Even Draven's furrowed brows softened.

"You summon your mother?" asked Ravana, missing the bigger issue at hand. "That can't be good for her soul." She examined her bright red fingernails.

"It's *fine* for her soul. I just have limited chances to talk to her before she can't come back." I really wished everyone would stop interrupting. "But Leana…"

"She didn't cross?" said Faine quietly, and this time, her somberness seemed especially warranted.

"When does *that* happen?" Draven asked. He sat back atop my potions table, bending one knee so his foot dangled off the ground, pointing inward.

I blinked hard, looking anywhere but at him.

"When a soul has unfinished business," Virginia explained for me. "But that's not the case for Leana. Or at least, she's not manifesting as a spirit here because of it."

"So where is she?" asked Draven.

"Virginia and I did some investigating, and I found this in Milton's attic." I brushed past the vampires and picked up the little flask containing red ectoplasm. Draven had nearly bumped into it.

"What is it?" asked my ex, his nose wrinkling.

Ravana eyed it quietly, her brow furrowing. She seemed almost mesmerized.

"Ectoplasm," I said.

"Isn't that usually green?" Faine pointed to the wall. Right. I had to clean that. But the way Ravana looked at the trail of green goo just then as if she could gag made me want to leave it right where it was.

"It is," I said. The flask felt heavy in my hand, so I put it back down. "And this stuff… It dampens my magic."

Draven whistled. "I didn't know that was possible."

"Neither did I," I admitted. Out of the corner of my eye, I checked him out in profile—the way his eyebrows drew together just slightly as he examined something reminding me too much of all the cute little things I'd once found attractive about him.

That I *still* found attractive about him.

Taking a deep breath, I stepped back.

"Do you have to drink it to feel its effects?" Ravana asked, peering around my shoulder to look at it.

"What? No." I stared her up and down. "You think I found evil red ectoplasm and *drank* it?"

She shrugged, her nose in the air. "I don't know how you witches operate. You drink potions, don't you?"

"Yeah, and they've never called for ectoplasm as a rule. Kind of a bad idea to include supernatural poisons in any concoctions, magic or not."

Ravana stepped back, offering me a clearly forced smile.

Draven picked it up, examining the bottle. He opened the cork and sniffed it. I didn't think he had much of a sense of smell.

"Do you feel anything?" I asked after a moment.

He shook his head, handing it toward Faine. "You?"

Her hand trembled as she reached for it.

"Faine, you don't have to," I started.

She shook her head and took a deep breath. "If this will help figure out something for Leana..." She took the flask from Draven and her nose wrinkled immediately. She shoved it back to him. "I didn't feel anything necessarily, but goodness, it's rank." Faine *did* have a heightened sense of smell. She waved her hand in front of her nose, steeling herself and swallowing as she turned away from us. "And it was warm."

I took the flask from Draven myself, my fingers touching his ice cold hand briefly before warming immediately with the flask. I sniffed it. It *did* smell bad, but it didn't hit me anywhere near as hard as it had hit Faine.

Broomie hovered closer, suddenly drawn to what we were doing, but she stopped, almost as if a force were keeping her from getting too close.

"Broomhilde?" I asked, making sure she was okay.

Shaking her bristles, she took off, settling atop the couch, the farthest she could get from the rest of us without disappearing from view.

"So it doesn't affect all paranormal creatures equally," said Draven.

"This is all well and good," said Ravana, "but seeing as how you don't seem to know much about that... *grime*, I suggest we don't keep that poor, confused old man waiting." A hand on her hip, she sauntered to the door.

Draven hopped down from the table, examining

his hand and offering me a knowing grin. He'd noticed I'd cleaned the table. *Bananaberries.*

"Shall we?" he asked.

Sighing, I put the flask down on the table. I didn't need to bring that with me, not if I was still uncovering the truth of what had happened to Leana—and those two unfortunate souls buried in my backyard.

Despite trying so hard to keep it a secret from the too-curious professor, I might need all the magic I could manage if Eithne had indeed had a hand in this.

Chapter Eleven

*A*fter an awkward dinner, made much better by the fact that even the worst of moods could brighten with some of Faine's home cooking, most of us settled into an area of Milton's living room where Cable had cleared some space. Milton's green gaming table was in the middle, a ragtag collection of kitchen chairs, folding chairs, and Milton's armchair around it.

"Seven of us, huh?" asked Cable, counting the chairs with a glass of sparkling water in his hand. "I wonder if we should split up, play two games?"

"Or find a game that includes us all?" asked Ravana aloud, more to herself than anyone else, as if that were the obvious solution. She and Draven hadn't eaten, feigning having had dinner at home during their awkward introduction. She stood in the kitchen, staring out the window that overlooked the backyard, not even turning to look at us.

Draven had sat on the back of the couch just watching us as we'd eaten and he hadn't moved a muscle since.

"Six of us," said Milton from his armchair, getting the number wrong. He sniffled, his stare hard. "Leana always wants to play bridge, but Abraham and I... We're all about the board games." He clapped his hands together. "So let's play the games!"

"Uncle, before we do, I found that album you wanted." Cable set his drink down and said, "Excuse me" to Draven, who only just slightly shifted, forcing Cable to stretch rather awkwardly across the pale man's leather jacket to retrieve a quilt-pattern-covered album. Cable blinked hard at Draven as he stood, shrugging when the vampire didn't say a word at the intrusion. Flipping through the album, he found a specific page and slid it on the green table in front of his uncle.

"Why, you're all so young!" said Virginia, peering over Milton's shoulder. She was so fixated on the picture, she didn't seem to notice that she leaned *through* Milton, leaving a little blob of green on his shoulder.

Fortunately, that wasn't where Cable was looking.

"Let me see!" I skipped over between them, patting Milton's shoulder to get the ectoplasm off, using a chance to look at the photo as an excuse. But my eyes really were drawn by the picture.

It was from the sixties or seventies maybe, the photo yellowing and cracked at the corner. Four adults posed around the same green table before us in this very same room, though there was no traces of a bed in the background.

Milton was easy to spot, so much like what he looked like now, only younger. Perhaps with more of a resemblance to Cable than I'd initially pinpointed, an easygoing attractiveness without an awareness of the effect his smile had on those around him. Beside him was Leana, as beautiful then as she had been when I'd known her, only with dark hair instead of dyed blond locks and prominent freckles across her nose.

Across from them were, I assumed, the neighbors who'd lived in my house. Jessmyn and Abraham. He was stout and stocky, a mustache making him look more severe than the mischievous smile on his lips would have otherwise conveyed. She was tall and willowy, with short, curly dirty blond hair held back with a headband, caught halfway between putting down the red wine glass in her hand and laughing. To the side of the board game was a half-eaten blueberry pie, a red Second Place ribbon hanging off the tin.

Milton ran a gnarled finger over Leana's face in the photo.

"Is that Clue?" asked Faine. I hadn't even noticed her sneak up on the other side of Milton.

"Oh, that must be Evidence," I said, leaning even closer to get a better look.

"Evidence?" parroted Ravana dryly, walking over to the rest of us.

"A Clue knockoff. We think." Cable rushed across the room and came back with the box he'd tucked away behind Milton's nightstand. "Dahlia *stumbled on* it in the attic." He smirked, an inside joke.

Okay, I was a little amused.

Draven jumped to the floor from the back of the couch with more force than necessary. "Then whip it out, young man. If I remember right, that should accommodate up to eight players."

Cable cocked his head at the vampire for a minute, though Draven pointedly refused to acknowledge him as he took the game from Cable's waiting hands. The "young man" remark, Draven's seeming familiarity with the game... His paleness, the red-rimmed eyes. I could see the gears in Cable's head turning too fast for my liking.

"The game," said Milton, letting out a sigh. He pushed the album away, and I slid it off the table for him as Draven set the game box down and removed the cover.

Cable joined Faine and Draven in setting up the board and pieces, taking it upon himself to shuffle the cards that would divine the who, how, and where of the crime at hand, if Clue was anything to go by. The house that made up the game board was a bit different than expected, still clearly a mansion, but more gothic and gloomy, with spiderwebs drawn in every corner, and at the center was a cartoonish pale blue butler with pointed ears and a widow's peak clearly meant to be the cookie cutter version of a vampire.

Draven stopped Faine from setting some game pieces out in the wrong part of the illustration, his knowledge of the little differences that made up this knockoff game surprisingly insightful.

Too insightful.

Stepping back, I almost bumped into Ravana.

"Check that album," she said quietly, a playful smile on her face. "Since you're so concerned about the poor boy seeing things he shouldn't."

Gulping, I flipped past that first Games Club picture and found just about what I'd imagined I'd find thanks to the cryptic nudge Ravana had given me.

The four members of Luna Lane's original Games Club. Joined by two more.

With thick, volumized hair and clothes more at home at a seventies costume party, Ravana and Draven sat at the green game table with the rest of them. On the couch behind the group was what looked a pile of several square-ish, leather bags in different colors, each with two handles. One was open and the three holes of a bright red bowling ball brought what I was seeing into focus. That was when the Luna Lane bowling alley had been open.

But more concerning than that observation were the two vampires front and center.

I knew the whole legend about vampires and mirrors, but that didn't apply to the vampires and photos. The last remnants of ashes in my fireplace from the burned photos of Draven and me could attest to that.

This photo showed the two of them unmistakably. And unmistakably having not aged a day since.

Squealing, I slammed the album shut.

"Oh, heavens, that Polaroid reminds me—I miss the old bowling alley. We'd usually bowl before club," she told me, her voice almost too quiet to hear. "That's right. *We*. It wasn't always four who played, despite Milton's fuzzy memories." Ravana let out a tittering laugh, which drew Cable's attention.

"Everything okay?" he asked.

"Peachy," I answered, twirling around. "EULG," I said as softly as possible to the album's pages. I didn't want to keep Milton from heading down memory lane, but I could safely magic away the stickiness later. When Cable had lost interest in it.

I tossed the album between the couch and the table beside it, then quickly, too eagerly, took a seat beside Virginia at the table. Mine was a kitchen table chair, and it was so old, it was a little wobbly. "So how do we play?" I chirped.

Faine took the seat beside me, and Draven's lips turned noticeably into a frown. Still, he took the seat beside her without comment, Milton on Virginia's other side, Cable beside Milton, and Ravana between her sired vampire and the visiting professor. She made a point of crossing her legs slowly, her eyes traveling up Cable's broad arms and to his neck.

"So you think you might move to town for good, handsome?" she asked.

Cable didn't react to her batting eyelashes, though Draven's expression grew even more sour, which apparently had been possible. Instead, Cable pulled a padded eyeglass sleeve out from his shirt pocket and slipped on his glasses. He looked even more attractive with the glasses on. I had to stare at the game to get my head on straight.

"No, unfortunately," he said, offering a little chuckle. "I don't imagine there are any openings for professors here."

"Not the kind who teach useless subjects," muttered Draven.

"I'm sorry?" asked Cable. He didn't seem affronted. It was more like he hadn't heard.

Ravana leaned toward her vampire progeny and gripped his upper arm, patting him gently like a little puppy in need of attention.

Draven lapped it up, flicking a bit of his hair over his shoulder like his vampire sire so often did herself. "Okay, the goal of this game is to be the first person to discover who killed the house's master." Draven pointed to the cartoonish doodle of a woman with long, gray hair in a violet dress, a giant set of pearls around her neck. Her eyes had Xs drawn across them, her tongue sticking out for comedic effect. She was near the bottom edge of the game board, cartoonish Scotland Yard-style policemen all around her. "We play as Lady E's guests, and one of us is likely the killer." He looked around to each of us dramatically. Faine laughed, and Virginia shook a little in her chair. A ghost afraid of murder.

Ravana tittered beside him. "I love it when the winner one round is the murderer the next. It's like the hero being corrupted and falling." Her dark eyes glistened and she licked her lips.

"So this knockoff is more popular than I thought." Cable eyed the vampires warily.

Draven finally looked straight at Cable and sent him a withering glare. I could see Cable making mental notes.

Everyone else's attention seemed affixed on the game. I gave it a closer inspection. The board depicted cartoon rooms in a mansion, all with a touch of the ghoulish. An attic full of spiderwebs and giant spiders, a greenhouse with a green-skinned gardener who had a bolt through his neck, and a master bedroom with a pair of skeletons under the sheets, for instance.

"So... How to determine the winner," continued Draven, unabated. "You explore the confines of the haunted mansion—"

"Does it have to be haunted?" asked Virginia.

He shrugged. "How else do you explain these?" With a black-nail-polished finger, he pointed out several spooky sheet-like ghosts drawn throughout the board.

"Not ghosts," said Virginia sullenly, sinking in on herself. "Maybe marshmallow men."

"Not ghosts," echoed Milton sadly.

"Yes, well…" Draven flicked his hair again. The eyeliner really brought out the red rims in his gaze. "Roll the dice, explore the rooms. Land on one of these spaces"—he pointed them out—"and pick a card. In the envelope there"—he pointed to an envelope I hadn't noticed between Cable and Milton—"is the solution. Which of us is the killer, what they used to do the killing, and which room the crime occurred in."

"It didn't happen right there?" Faine pointed to the body in the drawing of the great foyer.

There was something unsettling about the "Lady E" drawing. More than her being cartoon-ishly dead, of course.

"Nope," said Draven coyly. "The killer dragged her body out there."

"So with each evidence card you uncover, you can eliminate that person, place, or thing from your list." Ravana reached into the lid of the box and pulled out a stack of yellowing printed paper. Tearing off a top sheet, she passed the pad along and we all followed her example. Cable reached into a nearby desk drawer and pulled out a medley of pencils and pens, passing us each one, while Ravana continued. "The only ones not in play are in that envelope."

"The killer," said Milton softly.

Faine studied her sheet of paper, tapping the cap of her pen to her mouth. "So what do you do when you think you have it solved?"

"If you know who the killer is and how and where the crime was committed," said Draven excitedly, "you shout out the answers if it's still your turn."

A thought occurred to me. "And if you *are* the killer?"

The corner of his mouth twerked up. "You quietly, without trying to let anyone know, make your way here." He tapped the top of his pen to the backdoor right behind the policemen. "Escape outside, declare the truth, and you win."

"Or identify the killer and the where and the how to the police and you could also win," added Virginia, absorbed in following along.

"That's no fun," said Ravana. "But yes, that seems to happen more often than not."

So it was a lot like the game it was knocking off, but with just the slightest number of differences.

"There's one more piece of the puzzle missing," said Cable, that look on his face too similar to the one he had on when about to take notes.

It dawned on me. "You said if you're the killer

to quietly sneak away. Does that mean other players can catch you before you get away?"

Draven smirked. "Only if you at least know the where and the how at that time. Same for the killer —no escaping until you know the murder scene and the murder weapon. But if you're another player and you just *think* someone might be heading out the back door... You can't guess until it's your turn, and if you guess wrong, it'll be your last."

"Last what?" Virginia asked, gulping.

"Last guess," said Ravana. "Last turn." Her voice lowered. "The real killer will"—she sliced one long, delicate pale finger across her neck—"before you can ever guess again."

The room went silent, except for Milton murmuring his wife's name under his breath.

Then Draven and Ravana laughed, their accented maniacal cackles at home in the setting of the game.

As if to punctuate the sound, the sky cracked open with a flash of light outside, a distant rumble of thunder rumbling out behind it several beats later.

Chapter Twelve

"It was your fault, not hers!" shouted Milton over the thunder, to whom, I couldn't say. He was staring at the game board and rocking back and forth. "Yours, not hers. I wasn't wrong." He started sniffling and Cable patted his back.

Faine jumped out of her seat as the thunder continued to echo. "It wasn't supposed to storm tonight, was it?"

I chewed my lip as I stared out at Milton's backyard. I hadn't paid attention to the weather, but I could count on Faine to do so. Storms freaked her out.

She was emitting a little puppy-like whine under her breath just now as her hand dug into my thigh.

Cable stared across the table at us, scrutinizing Faine's reaction too closely.

"It's all right," I whispered to her, squeezing her hand back. "How close is it until…?" The full moon, I would have said, if Cable weren't so keen to overhear us just now.

"Tomorrow," she hissed.

Oh. I really did need to get my head out of my potions book and pay attention to things around me. The closer to the full moon, the more canine-like behaviors Faine and her family were likely to take on, and that included being terrified of storms.

"Well," said Cable, clapping his hands just as another sizzling flash of light and raucous rumble of thunder broke out. "Shall we begin?"

Faine started reciting a mantra under her breath. "I'm here, I'm in control, I'm safe. I'm here…"

"Faine, do you want to go home?" I whispered, thinking of her own comfort and of her kids'.

She shook her head. "Grady can handle them." She sat up straighter, but her hand began digging into her own thigh instead of mine. "I came here to play—and help you." She added that last part quieter.

Draven and Ravana, nonplussed by the raging storm, went about passing out the character cards.

I flipped mine over. Colonel Chicken Thigh. He wore all yellow and had a pointed goatee and a twirled moustache and an evil gleam in his bright blue eyes.

"Well, 'I' did it," I said. "Clearly."

Faine laughed nervously. "Don't be so sure." She showed me her card. Dame Sanguine. An elderly lady with a great black Persian cat on her lap, nails like razor-sharp claws, and a frilly dress more at home in Virginia's spectral closet.

She also had one of those faces… Well, if not for the haughty look, she'd seem sort of familiar.

All of the characters looked as dastardly. Virginia was Romario Sparklebreath, a black-haired, mustachioed silent movie star with flawless golden skin, high cheekbones, and an obnoxious smile. Milton had gotten Tiger Chains, a big game hunter practically popping out of his khaki ensemble and lugging a two-gauge shotgun over his shoulder. Cable was, suitably, Professor Snitnose, a wiry, thin woman with cats-eye glasses and a severe expression. In her hand she held a ruler with which she was clearly more likely to hit someone than measure anything. Ravana and Draven were twin children, apparently—Ravana the girl, Draven the boy. The menacing twins had silky, black hair and pale white skin, which sent a shiver down my back. They could have been vampires but for the fact that their gimmick seemed to be corrupting childhood toys into weapons. Dreadful Darling, the boy, held a base-ball bat dotted with bent nails. Decadent Darling's yarn doll had a knife sticking out of the back of it.

"This game is creepy," voiced Virginia, shuddering.

Milton whimpered as he stared at the board, but then, just as Cable went to comfort him, he shook off the extended hand and straightened up.

"Milton?" I asked. "Are you sure you don't want to play something else?"

He shook his head and tapped the character card in front of him. "We have to," he said simply.

Lightning flashed across the sky.

"Just something to calm my nerves!" Faine jumped up from her chair and ran for the kitchen, where a bottle of wine she'd brought along with dinner was still half-full. She poured herself a glass and stared out the window overlooking the backyard that Ravana had found so fascinating earlier.

"Who wants to go first?" Draven held up the dice between two long fingers.

"Wait," I said as my eyes glanced over my suspect sheet. "There can be up to eight players, and there's a suspect missing."

Ravana turned over a spare character card not assigned to anyone and shrugged. "If the killer is someone not in play, the game just doesn't have the oh-so-fun 'escape getting caught' aspect to worry about. But the odds of that are slim, the more players there are."

The last suspect was named Flowery Allspice.

And though the crooked grin and the harsh angle of her brow were entirely unfamiliar, there

135

was no mistaking the flowing red-orange hair and the pointed cap on her head, though hers was white instead of black, slightly different in shape.

My nerves felt raw, my skin on fire. I traced the outline of my stone scales on my arm.

Ravana stared at me, bemused, as if wondering if I regretted asking her to talk about that last suspect. Had she kept the character out of play on purpose?

Cable examined the character card closely. Too closely. "Is she an evil chef?"

Allspice. But the spice I thought of was cinnamon.

I squinted at the card closer. Maybe that witch's hat *could* be construed as an odd-shaped chef's hat. The cartoon brandished a cleaver, and that wasn't exactly witchy to begin with.

"She looks like Miss Poplar," said Virginia, entirely unhelpfully.

Faine took a sip of some wine as she hovered back by the table. "Nuh-uh. Cinnamon. Dahlia's mom."

We did look alike, but Faine was right. This was my mom. A brutish, twisted caricature of my mom. In a professionally made board game.

"Who made this?" I demanded to know, jumping from my seat and crossing the room to snatch up the game box. There was no publisher information on the back, no date of copyright.

It all looked professionally done, mass produced, but I couldn't believe in such a coincidence.

Mom hadn't lived in Luna Lane back when the first Games Club had been playing this game.

"Leana," said Milton softly, taking the box from my weak grip. He pointed to the drawing of "Flowery Allspice" on the back amid the rest of them.

My mom and Leana had looked nothing alike. There was nothing of Leana in any of these characters.

Just another mixed-up memory of the poor man.

I spun on Draven and Ravana. "Why didn't you tell me?" Draven practically slunk back at my harsh, assessing gaze.

"Tell you what, dear?" Ravana was entirely unaffected. She grabbed the dice out of Draven's hand and rolled them. "Five," she said simply, taking the little cardboard cutout of her character and plunking her five paces from the illustration of the drawing room starting point. She gestured to Cable beside her, but she kept her eyes locked on me. "Now did you want to play or discuss anything in particular?" Her eyelids batted at me. "It doesn't matter to *me* either way…"

Cable watched the silent conversation between us with too much interest.

Sighing, I walked around the table and sat down, Faine downing the last of her wine and setting it on the counter behind us before taking her seat again.

We began to play.

Gameplay went quickly the first few rounds, as our malcontent characters spread out throughout the manor on the board, unearthing clues and keeping our detective work secret from the other players.

Milton had gone particularly quiet, and Cable helped him play, so he was actually privy to twice the clues he was supposed to be.

I didn't see him taking advantage of the fact, though. Each time he or Milton crossed out a clue, he only did it on the proper game sheet. Still, that would complicate Cable's ability to nab the culprit fairly—if I even cared who won.

Virginia was slower to notice that than I was. "Now wait a minute," she said at last after Milton took a turn. "Why, Mr. Woodward, if you're helping your uncle like that, you're going to know more than the rest of us!"

"Ginny," said Faine. "It's fine." A little more color had returned to her cheeks as the storm grew more distant, the thunder and lightning less frequent.

"But it's *cheating*." Virginia huffily rolled the dice and moved her character piece a few paces, then leaned back and crossed her arms.

Cable held both hands up. "I promise only to act on information I gather during my turns alone."

Ravana laughed, trailing a finger up Cable's upper arm. "A man of honor, huh? Men with honor just taste so *sweet*."

I bit my tongue. Ravana was going to be Ravana and I had more important issues at hand than just keeping Cable from blowing the whole lid off the town's big secret.

"Virginia, we're doing this for Milton," I pointed out as I took my turn and eliminated Dreadful Darling from the suspect list on my sheet. My eyes flicked to Draven then. A muscle in his jaw worked as he seemed intent on staring at the board in front of him instead of Ravana flirting with Cable beside him. He didn't like her romantically, I knew, but the vampires were awfully *friendly* with one another as a whole, and there was something about Cable that had affected Draven before he'd even met him. Just his presence had been enough to unnerve him. It had to be the fact that another handsome fellow would be around to share the spotlight.

"I still say it's cheating." Virginia crossed her arms and pouted, sinking back into her seat as Faine took her turn. "What's the point of Games Club if we allow cheating?"

The point was to cheer up Milton, for Pete's sake, but that wasn't getting through to Virginia.

Draven took his turn quietly, without comment, crossing something off on his list after uncovering a clue in the illustrated kitchen. There were all manner of slimy creatures overflowing out of a bubbling pot in the picture.

"We're almost done, Ginny," said Faine. "It's getting late. Maybe next time we can split up and some of us can play with Milton while the rest play a different game."

Virginia narrowed her eyes at the ill old man muttering to himself and the friendly visiting professor with all the menace of a man too kind to hurt a fly. "This game doesn't count if either of the two of them win."

Ravana laughed and took her turn. She flipped over a clue in the cartoon mansion's private bowling alley.

Faine shook her head and leaned over toward me. "She doesn't like when any of my kids 'cheat,' either. They're *kids*. They don't always understand whatever games she wants them to play."

Virginia huffed, clearly having heard Faine's comment. "There's *no point* in not following the rules."

"Oh, I see what's going on here," said Ravana. "Then I'll stop you. The killer is—"

"Dame Sanguine!" shouted Milton out of the blue.

Cable reddened and whispered to his uncle.

I glanced at Faine, who slunk sheepishly into her chair. She'd visited some of the same rooms as Milton.

I looked at my own game sheet. It was down to

her and Tiger, according to my own deductions. Was Faine the "killer," and did she realize it?

I glanced at Faine's character card. Something sunk in the pit of my stomach. That face. It wasn't just "one of those faces." It was someone I knew. "Faine, does Dame Sanguine look familiar to you, too?"

Faine went very still, her lips slightly parted. "She does. But who...?"

"Dame Sanguine with the pillow!" shouted Milton. Then he clutched at his hair. "No, no, no. Doing it wrong."

Cable put a hand on Milton's shoulder. "Uncle, you still haven't uncovered *where* the crime took place..."

Virginia tossed her game sheet to the floor. "Well, the game's over. No point in this now."

Faine's character token was just a few spots away from the back door. Had she gathered all of the information? I'd never have suspected sweet, kindly Faine, but here she'd been, about to give us all the slip without a single tell.

"We're almost done," I said, nudging Faine.

She fluffed it off. "Oh, that's all right."

"Come on," I said. "Let's just finish this. Ravana?"

Ravana's eyes sparkled. "I suppose I don't *have* to solve the murder this round."

Milton launched himself over the board, picking up the dice.

"So you're passing?" Virginia sighed. "Milton? Cable needs the dice. It's his turn."

Milton stood and snatched his hand away, gripping on to the dice for dear life. "No! We're playing this wrong! You can't win!" He pointed one shaky, gnarled finger at Ravana.

"Sure. Stop the person about to *nab* the killer." Tittering, Ravana stood as well. "It *is* getting late, and I think we all know who did it now. Too bad. I was about to win."

"'About to' doesn't matter when there's rampant cheating," added Virginia, hopping up as well. Only, her movements were too fluid, more sliding right through the chair rather than standing up from it. Thank goodness Cable seemed distracted with calming down his uncle. "Do you see why we can't let people cheat now?" asked Virginia. She was already moving smoothly—too smoothly—toward the front door. "I'm leaving. Let me know if you ever want to play a proper game."

"Goodnight!" called Cable, but she ignored him. In just the nick of time I jumped up, blocking Cable's view of the door. Sure enough, I heard the telltale trickle of Virginia's ectoplasm sliding down the wood of the door rather than the door opening and shutting like it ought to have.

She really *did* get agitated over this cheating business. And had she forgotten the other aim of this evening? To find out clues—*real* clues to a real crime that might have taken place here?

"You can't win," said Milton, shuffling as quick as he could back to his bed, the dice still clutched in one fist. "Playing it wrong."

"Maybe it's best we all call it a night," Cable said. "Thank you all so much for coming—thanks again, Faine, for the delicious food."

"You're welcome," she said.

"Thanks for having us," I added, clearing my throat.

Ravana stepped up and glided over to Cable's side. "Perhaps I can help you calm Milton down before bedtime? Milton likes when I tuck him in. Don't you, Milton?" she asked, her voice as smooth as silk.

Milton stared at her blankly for a second and then hissed. Actually *hissed*, clutching the dice to his chest. "Bloodsucker! You can't have them! Keep your wily charms away from me, harlot."

"*Uncle!*" Cable seemed mortified.

Ravana's eyes sparkled. She clearly found this all amusing. "Keep your dice, Milton. I just wanted to say goodnight."

The grandfather clock in Milton's entryway struck eleven. Time really had flown.

And I'd accomplished absolutely nothing of import by sitting here and playing this game.

"So where'd you do it?" asked Draven, tossing his hair back over his shoulder as he stood.

Faine didn't seem to realize he was speaking to her at first.

"Oh!" she said, jumping to grab her empty wine glass and bring it back to the kitchen. "The attic." She gestured to the drawing in the corner of a spiderweb-covered attic at the top of the manor.

She froze as she spoke, and Draven stiffened.

Of all the coincidences, that shouldn't have mattered much, but it just brought home how we had more important things to concern ourselves with than cheating and cartoon characters.

"Let's go get ready for bed," said Cable, taking his uncle by the arm across the room. "See yourselves out?" he asked us all over his shoulder.

Draven's smile was so fake, if it were a painting, it would have been pegged as a forgery. "Will do." His voice dripped with false sincerity.

Cable didn't seem to notice. "You can keep the dice," he told his uncle, which seemed to be enough to get the man to acquiesce.

"The game's over?" he asked.

"Yes." Cable patted his arm. "The game's over."

"She didn't win?"

"No, Faine didn't escape and get away with it."

Milton frowned and put the dice in Cable's hand. "Play again. We have to play again."

"Okay, but not tonight, Uncle Milton." Cable tossed the dice at the game board and directed his uncle away. "Time for bed."

Did Milton want to play or not play? Had he just not wanted someone else to win? There was no trying to make sense out of a mixed-up man's mind.

Once the Woodwards shuffled down the hallway and the door to the bathroom shut, I picked up the card depicting my mother and showed it to the two vampires accusingly.

"*How?*" I asked simply.

Ravana nodded to the Dame Sanguine card, too. "That's Mrs. Flores. When she was younger than you might have remembered her. Still old, but younger."

"*Oh,*" said Faine, a rag in her hand as she washed her stemmed glass. She was too used to taking care of such things to leave it for others, even when she was a guest.

I snapped up the card. Sure enough. My memories of Mrs. Flores were hazy, but I could see it in the dark eyes, the high cheekbones.

"They weren't characters when we first played the game back then," said Draven simply.

Ravana's brow arched. "They were indeed characters. They just looked different." She shrugged.

"But what does this mean?" I held the character cards side by side.

"You're the witch, not us," said Ravana simply.

Magic. Of course.

My gaze darted to the murder victim drawn on the board. Lady E. With her long, silver hair that reached down past her back.

"Eithne." The name came out of my throat in a rush, prickling on my throat like the sharp edge of a knife.

145

Faine put the glass down on the counter with a bang, and a final, distant crackle of thunder rung out throughout the room.

"Eithne Allaway?" she said, her voice as soft as snow. "The witch who cursed you? Who murdered your mom?"

As if there could be any other.

Chapter Thirteen

"*H*elp me gather the game," I said, hushed. "Quickly, before Cable and Milton come out and notice it's gone."

Faine and Draven went to work, and Ravana moved, gathering a card here and a card there, but she hardly maneuvered with any urgency.

"I take it 'Lady E' looked different when you last played the game, too?" I asked her.

She shrugged and fluffed at a curl of her hair. "I don't remember. It was *so* long ago."

Draven glared at her. "I don't think she did. Not that there's much to go off of with that." He gestured at the illustration of the corpse, the Xs over the eyes taking up most of the face.

He, Faine, and I had most of it stuffed into the box in the next few seconds, Draven snatching the few cards Ravana had in her hands from her and stuffing them inside.

She clamped her lips together, as if mildly amused. "The game won't be nearly so exciting without a mad old man shrieking throughout the night."

I frowned at Ravana's insult of poor Milton. "I don't intend to play it. I want to check it for traces of magic."

Ravana laughed shrilly and put a hand on her hip. "I don't think you need to run any *tests* to decide it's no normal game."

"Even so. What else do I have to go on?"

The bathroom door opened. "Harlot, you get out of this house!" shouted Milton.

Ravana stiffened and walked right out the front door, no doubt insulted that he'd continued to address her by such a term.

She turned into a bat and flew off into the sky.

"Uncle Milton, *please*. You can't use that word. Come on now. Wash your hands."

Cable's voice echoed, followed by a toilet flush and the water running.

I had seconds before they got out here and asked for the game back or questioned why I had it tucked underneath my arm in the first place.

So I panicked, running for the open front door. I was out and down the front walk to the sidewalk before someone bothered to follow me.

Of course it was Draven. He shuffled up my front step beside me. "Faine is covering for you.

Your visiting professor noticed your backside rushing out the front door."

Good going, Dahlia.

But I had more important things to worry about.

Stepping inside my own home, I had to quickly set the board game down on the end table by the door to catch Broomie for her "welcome back" hug. I noticed a bucket of cornhusks on the kitchen counter. Goldie must have come over after the store had closed. Since she sometimes kept Broomie company for me, she was welcome to walk into my house whenever. I'd have to thank her, no doubt catch her up with everything that had happened now that the dust had settled.

Broomhilde wagged the end of her shaft eagerly, then her brush cocked up, staring over my shoulder.

Draven hovered in the doorway.

"You may come in," I said, and he stepped inside, shutting the door behind him.

A jittery sensation traveled up my spine. Draven and I alone. Here. In my house.

"How come I keep having to invite you?" I asked. "You used to come and go without waiting for such formal permission."

Draven fidgeted, tapping a finger against his thigh. "Intent," he said quickly.

"Pardon?" I stroked Broomie's bristles, the crackling sensation ticklish against my calloused fingers.

"Intent," he said, louder this time. He stared at me, sighing. "We don't need someone to outright say, 'Come in,' though most, like your sabbatical professor, usually do when you hover on their front doorstep. We just have to know whether or not we're welcome. It's a feeling. I can't describe it."

"Oh." I turned to put Broomie atop the couch. "Is that why Ravana left so quickly?"

"When Milton wanted her out? Yes." He shrugged. "Intent can shift on a dime. Or after months of a relationship slowly dying." His eyes looked glossy, and he walked over to offer Broomhilde a pat. She hesitated but shifted up to accept the contact.

We'd dragged our relationship on longer than we should have, maybe.

I'd still cared about him.

And that was all the brain power I could devote just now to that.

First slipping on my witch's hat, I snatched the board game off the table and crossed the open space, putting it down in the middle of the rune circle.

"So what's the plan?" he asked.

"I don't know yet." I flipped through my potions book. "I might need a boost before I can identify and unravel the enchantments on this game."

I started rifling through what potions I had ready, the rosewood out of stock but a similar pine-needle-based mixture on hand. I swallowed it and waited for the potion to take effect.

Draven moved closer. The air between us was practically tangible. If he moved one inch closer, he could lean in for a kiss.

His fingers moved toward my chin, and I knew, like an echo of what he'd done many times before, he was about to tilt my head up to meet his. "Dahlia, I—"

The door opened and it was a couple of seconds before I blinked, brought back to reality, and I thought to turn my head and look at who'd let themselves in. Faine was shutting the door behind her, paying us little mind just yet. She probably didn't want to disturb any enchantments I'd begun casting.

And instead of casting enchantments, I was standing here, a hair's breadth from Draven's dark red lips…

"I told him you had to get home, and that you took the game for my kids," she said. "I didn't want him to wonder where it had gone off to—" She froze. Faine stared at Draven, then at me, as if she'd just walked in on something she wasn't supposed to see.

I jumped back, putting more space between Draven and me.

"Virginia's not here?" she asked, clearing her throat. "Where'd she go?"

"Who knows?" I smoothed a lock of my fiery-orange hair, and I felt a chill across my face, my hair whipping upward. It reminded me of a huff of breath.

"What was that?" I asked.

"What was what?" asked Draven.

"Oh. Okay. So I should probably check in on the kids," Faine said after a beat. "I just thought I'd see what you found out, if anything…"

"Stay," I commanded, and like a dog, she went rigid in place. "Er, I mean you *can* stay. This shouldn't take long."

"All right." She studied Draven's face. I didn't have time to think about what his clenched jaw could mean.

Faine leaned back against the couch, petting Broomhilde, while Draven just stood where he was, his arms crossed tightly over himself.

I was wrong. It took very long indeed.

I was drifting off as I muttered every relevant word I could think of backward, but nothing was happening.

An hour later, Faine excused herself, wishing me the best and apologizing, but she had to make sure the kids had gone to bed all right, especially considering the errant storm.

The mention of the storm sent me wildly down another train of thought. It hadn't been forecasted. That could mean a disturbance in the ley lines around the area.

I flipped through the potions book, completely

oblivious that with Broomie's soft snoring from the couch, that meant that Draven and I were well and truly alone. The sudden realization hit me and I twirled around.

"You're still here?"

He smirked. "I thought you wanted help solving the mystery of Leana's possible murder."

"Yes. Yes, of course…" Of all the people in town I'd asked for help, he was the only one who'd stayed. Not that I faulted Faine, of course. But Ravana and Virginia…

"The game," he said.

"What about it?"

"Does it really matter where it came from?"

I spun on him. "My mom told me Leana didn't cross over, Milton uncovered two dead bodies in my backyard, and you ask me if—" I stopped myself. Okay, I didn't actually see the immediate connection. But what else did I have to go on right now? "Leana played this game," I said feebly. "It clearly has traces of magic in it."

"So you think… the game killed Leana?"

"I don't know!" I snapped. "It's a strange coincidence otherwise that she died in the attic, where this thing was oozing out red goo. My mom felt Eithne's magic in town, and the unpredicted storm could indicate she's up to something. If she's at minimum responsible for my mother's and Mrs. Flores's faces in this game, then it's worth looking into." My voice went quieter, my fingers quaking at my side. My muscles still ached from all the digging earlier today.

"Is it so awful that Eithne would enchant a game?" he asked quietly.

"*Yes*," I snapped. As if that needed to be said. I turned on him. "Anything she had a hand in can only spell trouble. So forgive me if the strange things in this game make me suspicious. And if anyone knew she was in town and so much as *held the door open* at Vogel's for her, let alone told her about this game and got her to mess with it and put Leana and Milton in danger, I'll turn them into a frog and keep them in a one-foot-wide aquarium for the rest of their days!" I was breathing heavily now.

His mouth opened, then shut. "You're tired," was all he said to my outburst.

I checked the clock. Five A.M. I'd been at this all night and *nothing*. Like it was nothing more than a normal board game. But that couldn't be right.

"You used to be a night owl." He leaned one forearm against the wall. "Other than your daily good deed."

"Not lately," I bit out. Not since I had to stay up all night or miss out on time with my boyfriend.

His brow furrowed as he examined my potions-mixing table.

"Dahlia, did you move that *red goo*, as you put it, far enough away?"

I spun. There it was. The flask in question, the red, oozing ectoplasm.

"Oh, bananaberries!" I swore, shoving the flask at him.

He stumbled a little but took it nonetheless. His eyes sparkled with mischief. "You forgot about that, didn't you?"

I didn't want to admit I'd been so foolish. But of course I had. I'd been so focused on the game...

I spent my days brewing potions, cutting grass, washing cars—those types of things. I wasn't cut out to be a detective.

"It doesn't affect you that we know of," I said, massaging my temple. "So can you take it far away? Don't *lose* it, but just take it away."

The flask glowed menacingly in his hand. "If it were up to me, I'd lose this somewhere outside Transylvania. Keep it far, far away."

"You do feel something?"

"Well, no. Nothing I can quite name. But it just..." He stared at it and swallowed. "It's doing *something* to me. And I don't like the look of it."

Me, neither.

"Do me this favor then?"

He sighed. "All right. But only because you haven't asked me for anything in a long time. A *long* time."

If he was hinting I should have been swinging by his pub more often, asking him for favors, I couldn't say I agreed with him.

"It's okay for *you* to ask for help sometimes, too, Dahlia," he added.

155

That was becoming a familiar refrain.

"Thanks," I said, doing my best to put on a flittering smile. "Just keep it at your place for a day or so—I'll let you know what, if anything, I find."

He looked at the clock. "Sunup is soon enough. I won't make it back until this evening."

"I'll update you," I promised. "As soon as you wake."

He frowned but sashayed over to the door. "*As soon as* the sun sets," he reiterated. "Be careful," he added after a beat. "And you get some rest, too."

He stood there awkwardly a moment more and then nodded, opening the door and turning with a puff of smoke into a flittering black bat, clutching the small flask with his claws.

I shut the door behind him and let out a great, big sigh that echoed around the room, almost like someone was sighing with me.

I needed to focus. Shaking my head to clear it, I strode across the room and to the board game, an idea already coming to me.

"DNIB!" I said, calling on all the magical energy around the room to bind itself to the game. A little squeak rang out in the room, and I checked over my shoulder to make sure Broomie was okay. She was still sleeping. It must have been a reaction to a dream she was having.

Nothing about the game seemed any different, though it trembled a little at the enchantment. Perhaps I *had* collected the energy toward the game.

"STERCES RUOY LAEVER," I said, both arms held out toward it. "RETSAC CIGAM RUOY WOHS!"

And like a light switch turned on, my powers activated, the rune circle glowing as the board game began floating in the middle of it.

The top of the box came out and cards and pieces all twirled around in the air.

I kept my aching arms steady, overcome by the sudden overflow of power, trying as hard as I could to hold on to it all.

The lights in my house flickered and then went out with a crackling zap. Broomhilde cried out, growling as she sprung awake, but I couldn't offer her any comfort, couldn't stop the magic from running wild.

The door blasted open, the embers of the dawn trickling into the dark house lit only by the glowing rune circle.

All the magic stopped, the game clattering to the ground, the lights flickering back on, my arms heavy and exhausted.

"It's about time you were alone," said the goddess-like woman with the pointed lilac hat who was standing on my front porch. "Present company excepting, of course," she added to Broomhilde. My broomstick cowered and sunk behind the couch.

Her long, silver hair fluttered as her black broomstick charged into the room, darting for

Broomie's bucket of cornhusks and chomping down like it owned the place. Broomie whimpered.

"Hello, Dahlia," said Eithne Allaway, the slightest hint of an Irish accent to her words. "You called for me?"

Chapter Fourteen

"*I* didn't… I'd never…" I couldn't form a complete sentence, my thoughts a jumble in my head.

She was here, standing before me.

The witch who'd cursed me.

The witch who'd murdered my mother.

She hadn't shown her face since.

Yes, my mom had told me she'd sensed her magic in town, and yes, I'd suspected she was up to no good, but to come face to face with her now…

"What are you doing here?" My fingernails dug into my palms as my fists shook at my sides.

"You asked the magic caster on that game to reveal herself, so here I am." Eithne took a few steps inside, and the door slammed shut behind her, though she hadn't said a word. She didn't need to speak her enchantments aloud.

She just needed to *think* an evil thought and it was done.

"Hmm," said Eithne, looking around. "I like what you've done with the place. Especially outside. *Messy.* Makes it seem more befitting a witch, especially one just a hop, skip, and a jump away from turning to stone." Both her shoulders rose and fell, a broad grin on her face. "A fitting resting place for a spooky statue all the town kids can come dare each other to visit, don't you think? 'Beware the witch frozen in time.'"

My hand subconsciously rubbed at my stone scales. There was so much I wanted to say to her, so much I wished I had the power to *do* to her. But there was something important she'd said.

"You admit it. You cast the enchantment on this game." I went over and started picking up the pieces, brandishing the card of Flowery Allspice in the air. "Why does this look like Mom? What did you do to Leana?"

"One question at a time, my sweet gargoyle," she said. I winced at the insult. I'd never seen a gargoyle in person, but they weren't the most attractive of stone statues. At least they weren't actual living creatures, like they could be in some stories. Or at least I thought anyway. What did I know? If a paranormal creature didn't come here, I didn't meet it.

Eithne hopped up and sat on the edge of the couch, crossing her legs and clasping her hands atop her knee, her back rigid. Broomie scampered out from around the couch, hugging the floor until at my feet. To make her feel safer, I bent down and picked her up near the top of her shaft, the default position for a broom, offering her strength where she might otherwise have never have found it.

"Where's Leana?" I asked, with more gusto this time.

"Dead, last I knew." She gave me a half-shrug. "Didn't you go to the funeral? I saw you there, you know."

My spine grew stiff. "You were there?"

She stretched out a hand and picked up an unread magazine caught between the flowery couch cushions. "Not there, but I was watching. I'm always watching Luna Lane, my pet."

Don't let her distract you. I grit my teeth. "Leana didn't cross over."

Eithne looked up from the magazine open at her lap—a gardening magazine. An impulse buy a few months back. I'd thought that someday I'd find the strength of mind to fix up Mom's work with the garden in the backyard. "You don't say?" she said.

"And *I* think it has something to do with that game." The suspect card still in my hand, I pointed with it to the game on the floor, scattered about.

"Brilliant deduction." Eithne licked her finger and turned a page.

My muscles quaked. I itched to knock that magazine to the floor.

"Was that your ectoplasm?"

"Was *what* my *what*?" Her head shot up. She looked affronted. "Darling, I'm an enchantress, not a ghost."

"You're a witch." I pouted. "You just fancy yourself better than the rest of us."

"The rest of... who?" Eithne shook her head. "Have you ever even met a witch besides me or your mother?"

"Don't talk to me about my mother."

"All right, then. I won't tell you why the card changed to look like her." She turned another page in the magazine.

Even Broomie was quivering in my hand now, and it wasn't just from fear. Eithne's broomstick— I'd never known its name—stuck its bristles out from the bucket of cornhusks and let out a little burp.

Broomhilde went stiff immediately, cowed once more.

"Must you be so cryptic?" I snarled.

"My sweet child, what's the fun in me handing you all the answers?" Her violet eyes positively gleamed.

"Did you kill Leana?" I asked, desperate for whatever twisted answers she'd give me.

"No."

Unlikely.

She shut the magazine and gave me a onceover. "You don't believe me."

"You admitted your enchantments are all over this game."

"I did."

"Magic had to be involved in Leana's death... or she would have crossed over. Or stayed here as a specter at the very least."

"If you say so." She uncrossed and re-crossed her legs, this time at the ankles.

Another thought occurred to me. "And the skeletons in my backyard?"

Eithne's eyes lit up. "Exciting find, isn't it?"

She positively *reveled* in it.

"Milton knew where they were buried."

"And the first thought you have is that *I* must have killed them." She *tsked*. "You're looking past what's right in front of you."

"Right in front of me?" I scoffed. "Who else would be capable of such a thing? No one even knew—"

I stopped myself.

Milton had known.

He'd known exactly where those bodies had been buried.

And not for one second had I thought that meant he must have buried them there. That if that were true, then he'd probably even murdered them.

Eithne giggled, the sound so soft and feminine and not at all suited to a wicked witch.

"Milton couldn't have..." I took a few steps

163

back. "He's just a nice old man. He ran Vogel's before Goldie and Arjun. He'd never…"

"And *whose* wife died so mysteriously?" She wriggled her fingers in the air.

"If you're saying he killed *Leana*…! But he's not in his right mind anymore. I don't think he could have…" My mouth was dry. "Besides, that wouldn't explain why her soul went missing. Unless he's not human?"

"He's human," said Eithne quickly. "And so was his wife. And so were those two victims keeping the worms company in your mother's overgrown garden."

I wanted to believe she was lying to me—but I didn't know what I wanted to be the lie.

But Eithne, she got so much joy out of toying with me. Games were only fun if they were rooted in at least some truth.

"Who were they?" The words were scratchy against my throat.

"My dear pet, if you can't figure out *that* much…" She shook her head. "And here I'd thought you had a plan since you so ingenuously *bound* your supercilious friend to aid in a more *intimate* investigation of the game."

Supercilious? Intimate? Was that some crack about Draven and me and how awkward it had been for the two of us to be alone? How long had she been spying on me?

She didn't wait to let me ask her to clarify. I didn't know if I wanted to.

"I'll give you a hint. Or maybe two." She tilted her head back and forth. "*You* never met them, but you've seen them. The only two people in Milton's life who—"

"Jessmyn and Abraham," I said quickly, the truth dawning on me like a bolt of lightning. So much for waiting for the coroner's report for any clues.

"There you go, dear one."

The other two members of the Games Club. They'd supposedly moved away before Mom and I had moved in. Abraham had moved away to go into politics but probably had never been elected... Because he'd never gone into politics at all. He'd never left Luna Lane, and neither had Jessmyn.

"If you're wondering how your mother bought this house from a dead couple, I might have finessed some details with my enchantments. Made it seem like the happy couple had moved on, sold their house. Your mother got a *steal* by the way, and I funneled that money right back into her pockets. She never did keep a close eye on the piles of cash she stored in the other dimension. Do *you*, now that you're in charge of it?"

No. Not really at all. I asked for the cash and it appeared to me, so long as I asked for it from this rune circle.

"Back up," I said. "You were in Luna Lane back then?"

"I was. How else did you think your mother found this place? We were friends once, you know." She jumped back down to the ground, her hand out, and her black broomstick flying right back into it.

"*Friends?*" My throat went dry. Mom had always danced around the subject of her relationship with Eithne. She'd never wanted to talk about it.

"Once upon a time," said Eithne dryly. "A story for another day."

I could ask Mom next time I summoned her. Hopefully get a straighter answer out of her than I would out of this wicked witch.

"I'd hate to have had a friend like you," I spat. "So you were here. That just makes you more suspicious in my book. You said you helped *cover up* the Davises' deaths?"

"I did. But I didn't kill them."

I didn't understand why she would admit to one thing and not the other—unless it really was the truth. She was just as vile as I'd had every reason to believe. She just hadn't necessarily been the sole player at work in *this* tragedy.

Eithne swirled her broomstick toward me and a card shot up from the ground and into her hand. She held it up. Madam Sanguine.

"I said I wouldn't comment on *that* card at your

166

request, but I suppose I can give you a hint with this one. Recognize it?"

"Mrs. Flores." I scowled.

"Got it in one." She beamed. I wanted to smack that smile right off her perfect, forever-twenty-something-year-old face.

Okay, so I hadn't gotten that one on my own.

"Why is Mrs. *Flores* in the game?"

"She's not." Eithne shrugged and blew on the card. It languidly floated back toward the box on the floor and all the pieces—the card in my hand included—began shaking, flying back neatly and settling inside the game box. "Neither is your mother, but you know that. You talked to her less than twenty-four hours ago."

Mom. I clutched Broomie with both hands for comfort and to keep myself from launching at Eithne.

"I'll give you these three clues, my sweet little stone child." Eithne held up three fingers just as the top of the game box closed.

"One. You should play the game to completion. Let Milton put up a fuss. Let him sit out a round. Whatever. But someone needs to play." She bit her lip a moment as if to fight her smile. "Two. You should take a hint from that game and figure out the *how* and *where* they all died before you worry so much about the *who*."

I opened my mouth to speak, but Eithne continued undaunted.

"And three." She pouted. "You really need to take better care of yourself. You haven't slept a wink all night. Sweet dreams, my little gargoyle." She blew me a kiss.

I lifted Broomie in the air, trying to stop her.

But I was too late. Not even a single syllable escaped my lips before I collapsed to my knees and then to the ground, lost in the sweet release of slumber.

Chapter Fifteen

I pushed aside the rough, ticklish prodding of Broomie's bristles across my nose.

Just a few more minutes…

She let out a little trill and poked my side.

I bolted upright. I was lying in my bed, the covers still tucked in beneath me, my witch's hat hung on the corner of my knotted oak dresser.

"What time is it?" I whirled to get a look at the cuckoo clock Mom had brought along with her when she'd moved here.

Almost five o'clock. I ran to the window and drew back the curtain. In the evening. I'd slept for almost twelve hours straight.

"No, no, no," I said, slapping my hat on and brushing my hands over my outfit. "NAELC," I said quickly, everything from my black dress to my hair growing soft, fresh, and silky.

Broomie floated beside me as I trudged down the hallway.

"Thank you," I told her, patting her head. She shook, bending her handle to point inward at herself. She wanted me to take her on a ride.

"Not right now," I said, my stocking feet slapping against the hardwood floor. "I have to make sure…" The Evidence game was right where Eithne had so carefully left it, perfectly tidy on the floor in the middle of my rune circle.

I scooped it up.

The front door opened and in walked Goldie. Broomie zipped over to her, eager to see if she'd brought any more cornhusks.

Goldie stroked Broomie underneath her brush, where one might consider her chin, and picked a small bunch of husks out of her pocket. "Dahlia, dear, how are you doing?" Broomie's munching filled the house. She shuddered. "Those skeletons found in your backyard—"

I took Goldie's hand, giving it a grateful squeeze. "Could you take Broomie with you?"

Broomhilde's brush shot up.

"I need to check on Milton," I explained to her. "Remember about Cable?"

"Of course I don't mind. She can come back with me to the shop." Goldie eyed the game box I kept tucked under my arm. "What's that? One of Milton's?"

"Yes," I said, not sure how much to tell her. *"Play the game to completion,"* Eithne had said. It seemed a dangerous proposition, and Goldie was just a human.

So who was best to ask? Faine was obvious. But she had kids and... Wasn't it the full moon? Cursing, I tapped my foot, then remembered to slide it into my ballet slipper.

Virginia was the least in danger. I hoped.

Where was that ghost when I needed her?

Draven, Ravana, and Qarinah would probably be the next least vulnerable. Though I had quite a few questions for the older two vampires now that I knew whose bodies had been buried in my backyard —and the fact that Eithne claimed to have been in Luna Lane all those years ago. But they would have to wait until after the sun set.

The *sunset*!

"I haven't done a good deed yet!" I cried, slipping my other shoe on.

Goldie looked aghast. "Well, come on, then, come back with me to Vogel's. There's some stocking to do and oh... I did that. Um, Arjun has been wanting someone to shred some old documents of his. But we don't have a shredder and you can't use your enchantments." She curled her index finger against her lips. "You can use scissors?" she offered hopefully.

Oh, never mind. I could stand one more scale. Part of one arm was still so little of my body.

"No time," I said, giving her a quick hug with my one free arm. "But thank you." I dashed off.

It wasn't until I was nearly to the sidewalk that Goldie's voice carried out from my front porch.

"Dahlia Poplar, you do your good deed! You need to take care of yourself!"

Perhaps. But every minute I delayed was a minute more Leana's soul—and probably Abraham's and Jessmyn's, for that matter—dallied in who-knew-where. I hoped it wasn't a place of suffering.

My feet carried me next door before I'd even formulated my plan. No way were Cable and Milton playing this game with me, but I had to check in on them.

I had to look into Milton's eyes and *know* if he was capable of murder.

I knocked. And waited. No one answered.

I peered in through a crack between the drapes on the front window. "Hello?"

Under my breath, I said softly, "EVOM," indicating with my hand for the drapes to spread a little wider.

The rumble of an engine pulling into the driveway made my back stiffen and I spun around.

The door to the tiny tan smart car opened and out stepped Cable, almost comically too large for the vehicle.

Except the expression on his face… It was like he'd seen death.

"Cable!" I fled down the stairs. "What happened?"

He blinked hard, almost as if it took him an extra few seconds more than it should have to realize I was standing in front of him. "Dahlia." He smiled just a little, but it seemed a struggle. "Nice hat."

I winced but didn't comment.

Cable's smile was short-lived. "Milton's in jail."

What had I missed? Oh, curse that witch!

I turned on my heel, clutching the game even harder in my fingers. I had to talk to Roan.

The rushed footfalls falling in place behind me on the sidewalk leading downtown were punctuated by Cable's uneven breaths. "Aren't you wondering why?"

I shook my head, plodding onward.

"You guessed, then, that it had to do with those two bodies in your backyard." Cable sighed. "I don't know what to tell my mom. I'll have to call her, but I don't know how to even begin."

We walked on, and I didn't say a word. The more this visiting professor hung around me, the more danger he was in.

"Out of the blue, Milton told me it was time he 'dug them up,'" said Cable quietly, falling in lock-step beside me, continuing the conversation as if I'd posed questions. "At first I thought it was one of his episodes, though I have to admit the fact that he knew where to look for them…" His face went grim

173

and I focused back on the path in front of me. "And I thought, well, the sheriff seemed nice when I met him coming out of the pub yesterday. Real small-town. No offense."

He must have noticed me bristling.

"I thought he would talk him down. But when we got there, the sheriff was putting on his jacket, a piece of paper in his hand. It was a warrant. He said the IDs on those bodies came in already, cross-referenced with missing persons reports filed outside of town and—"

"His neighbors. The ones who owned my house before us."

"Yeah." Cable sent me a questioning look. "Milton was a person of interest, seeing as how he was the last one to see them. I didn't know those friends were *missing*, let alone..." He stopped himself. "But how did you guess?"

I halted, my feet suddenly heavy like lead. "Just a gut feeling," I said by way of excuse.

I didn't know if Cable bought it.

We were standing outside of the sheriff's office now, a small, brick building just a few blocks down from the pub and café.

"But Milton just *confessed*," Cable said. "He claimed he killed those neighbors decades ago... Wouldn't say why, but he insisted he'd acted alone. I tried to point out he has dementia, but the sheriff thought it best just to put him in the holding cell until it was all straightened out."

I barged inside.

"We're closed," called out Roan's deep bass from farther back inside. It was past five now, a patch of skin on my upper arm itching as the sun fled down past the horizon. "If it's an emergency—"

"You said you're never closed for me." Slamming the board game down on the front desk—empty, Sheriff Roan worked alone—I jumped over the swinging half-door dividing the entryway of the station from the rest of it and maneuvered around the filing cabinet to the back, where the building's single holding cell was located. The door was open, and Sheriff Roan, deep, purple bags under his eyes, was on a chair beside the pristine, white cot on which Milton was sitting. He clutched the edge of the cot and rocked, uttering his wife's name past tight lips. His hair was even more wiry than usual, his expression gaunt and haunted.

Cable came to a skidding halt behind me. "Uncle! He looks even worse than before." Without waiting to be asked, he slipped past me and switched places with Roan, Roan letting out a heaving sigh and following me out to the front of the building.

"You're jailing *Milton*?" The words were practically a screech in my mouth.

He lifted both hands in surrender. "I had no choice, Lia. County sent down a search warrant, and then he confessed. I had to hold them off, promise I could tackle this on my own, but they won't stay away much longer."

Crossing my arms, I scratched at the patch of skin. It was growing redder. "So what can you do?"

"There're some mental health people—"

"*No*," I said sharply.

Roan looked taken aback. "I want him home as much as anyone. But the county authorities are involved, and frankly, his disorder is the best defense he has—"

"For what? A sentence in an institution instead of a prison? That won't excuse whatever happened back then."

Roan checked over his shoulder, but Cable was talking to his uncle, paying us no heed. "Do you *know* what happened?"

"That's what I'm trying to find out." I grabbed him by the elbow and drew him closer to the front door. After a couple of minutes, I'd relayed everything I knew so far.

Roan let out a soft, slow whistle. "Leana? But if *she* was murdered—"

"We don't know that," I pointed out. I was suddenly defensive, worried Roan would pin the blame for that, too, on Milton. "Just that she's missing. Her soul is."

"Either way, it points to foul play. Whether of a variety Milton had a hand in or…"

"Someone else in town." My mouth set in a grim line. Someone else who couldn't have been just human. "I need to find out how and where the neighbors died."

"I can tell you the how," said Roan, scratching his cheek. His eyes seemed especially haunted and sunken with the movement. "Or at least tell you all I know. The autopsies point to blunt force trauma to the backs of the heads. For both of them."

"Both of them?" I wondered how the killer had managed to kill them both so quickly and take them *both* by surprise from behind. Had it been a team of two working together? Had the victims been killed in separate locations? "Anything else the autopsies told you?"

Roan shook his head. "The bodies were very decomposed, as were the clothes. The male was wearing a bowling shirt and corduroy pants, the female a cotton dress."

"A bowling shirt? Was there a team name on it or anything?"

Roan shook his head. "Just a basic bowling ball and pin design, as far as the investigators could tell. It was also decomposing. The only other thing the autopsies found of note was that in the bone matter, they both seemed somewhat deficient in a number of vitamins and minerals. D, B12, iron…"

"What does that mean?" I cocked my head. "They didn't eat right? Or they were poisoned?"

"Maybe their diet was lacking," said Roan. "But it doesn't point to poison." He went silent a moment. "You mentioned *where* they were killed. You don't think in the backyard?"

I shook my head. "Milton and Leana must have moved them there."

"Leana, too? Milton insisted he acted alone, and Leana isn't here to see any punishment, if she was involved…" Roan frowned, tapping his gut with one hand. "I can't picture little Leana having the strength to carry bodies anywhere. But I *can* picture Milton lying even just to protect her legacy. You don't think the witch who cursed you did it? Or compelled them to?"

Roan didn't know about Eithne's role in Mom's death. Faine did because I'd had to tell someone. Most people probably had an idea. But I'd never been able to tell Roan—he'd been so devastated. If he suspected, he never put voice to it, in any case. Absentmindedly, I scratched my elbow. "No. I don't think she was lying about that." Though I only had my gut to go on.

My eyes darted to the Evidence game on Roan's front desk. "Draven and Ravana. They knew Jessmyn and Abraham. They played this game with all of them. I need them to finish the game with me all the way through."

Roan checked his watch. "Well, it's almost suns—"

I didn't hear the rest of what he said over the sounds of the scream that ripped out from my own mouth.

"Ugh!" I mumbled, the skin on my upper arm growing red. The patch was large—the diameter of a baseball easily.

"Dahlia?" came Cable's voice, followed by the shuffle of his feet.

"Lia!" Roan stepped in to steady me.

Gritting my teeth, I fought through the pain as the stone scale wove its way onto my flesh.

"Lia." Roan's eyebrows folded inward. "Did you miss your good deed?" His voice was quiet, thankfully, because Cable appeared just then on the other side of me.

Locking eyes with Roan, I nodded grimly.

He looked... disappointed.

"What's wrong?" asked Cable.

"Nothing," I said, swatting at the air and stumbling backward. I needed to get steady on my two feet.

That evil witch had made me sleep all day on purpose—and not just to stop me from getting to the bottom of Luna Lane's most horrific secrets.

Roan's eyes went wide at the sight of the new scale on my upper arm and he slipped his jacket off the back of the nearby chair, wrapping it around my shoulders. I slipped into it gratefully, reminding myself to wear long sleeves in the future before Cable noticed that my *tattoo* was in the habit of spreading up and outward on my flesh like some kind of virus.

"Charley horse," I said, trying my best to smile. Cable didn't seem to buy it.

The three of us were silent for a bit, the only voice Milton's from the back, where he hauntingly called out his wife's name.

"Is that my uncle's game?" asked Cable, when it was clear I had no more to say on the subject of my outburst. "Did you get to play it with the kids?"

Lost for a moment, I suddenly remembered Faine's cover story. "Oh, uh, not yet. I was on my way…" I explained.

Bananaberries. On any other full moon, I really *would* have been on my way. Faine and Grady could usually handle it, but getting overrun by the werewolf sides of themselves *and* making sure the kids, who had far less experience and restraint, behaved themselves was a little too much for them to juggle. A witch's enchantments could always come in handy for keeping a toddler, a kindergartener, and a surly seven-year-old safely confined to their backyard.

"I have to go," I said suddenly, grabbing the game off the table.

Roan let out a sharp hiss of breath. "The café closed early today…" He was putting two and two together, too.

I whirled on him. "Tell Draven and Ravana I'm stopping by later. And send Virginia to their place, too, if you come across her. We have to play the game."

Roan looked over his shoulder. "But Milton…"

Cable's head bobbed from the sheriff to me, the gears in his head turning as he tried to keep up with our half-spoken conversation. "I can stay with Milton."

Good. Stay inside tonight. Stay locked away.

Roan nodded grimly. "I'll be back, son." He tossed him a ring of keys and Cable just barely managed to catch them, clutching them to his chest. "Keep the door locked, will you?" he asked as he snatched his tan, broad-brimmed sheriff's hat off the coatrack and affixed it atop his head.

And with that, the two of us headed outside, our destinations right next door to each other.

Chapter Sixteen

a shiny, classic red Ferrari pulled up beside us as we rounded the corner behind the café and pub and approached the two houses of the proprietors located side by side. The passenger's side window rolled down. "Sheriff!"

Mayor Abdel leaned out of the car, his great-great-great-etcetera granddaughter, Chione, behind the wheel. Chione's eyebags were still far too purple, like working at the small-town town hall was even more harrowing than the day of revelations that Roan had faced to earn his bags—the ones about murder and an old friend being a suspect.

"Mayor Abdel." Roan tipped his hat at him.

Abdel's usually friendly expression was grim. "We have to talk about this *murder* in town. Sad business. Sad, sad business."

With a jolt, I realized Abdel, like Draven and

Ravana, would have known Jessmyn and Abraham, too.

"Mayor Abdel?" I rushed to the curb, resting my free hand on the open window. The other still clutched the game at my side. "Did you know them?"

Abdel looked taken aback by my nearness. We weren't particularly close friends, though I performed good deeds for town hall as often as I did for anyone.

"Jessmyn and Abraham Davis," Roan explained. "The victims buried in our Dahlia's backyard."

"Oh, yes, of course." Abdel grew quiet, the smooth rumbling of his car engine filling the silence. "We all believed they'd moved. I was *sure* I remember them packing their things and telling us Abraham was off to get into politics. Despite the fact that he worked at town hall, he never aimed for *my* position, of course." He'd worked at town hall?

Abdel massaged his temple, mussing aside just a couple of strips of his mummy wrappings. I caught a glimpse of the face I so rarely saw in full—handsome, mustachioed, with high, sharp cheekbones. Those enchanted mummy wrappings keeping him alive for so long also apparently preserved him surprisingly well underneath. "But now I hear there was a report that they'd never shown up at their destination? A niece or something eventually reported them missing, but no one ever showed in

Luna Lane to investigate." He smoothly readjusted his wrappings so they covered most of his face.

"That was Eithne," I said quickly. "She told me she helped cover up their deaths. It's a difficult enchantment, one I haven't yet mastered, but it's possible to change memories." If I *could* easily perform the enchantment, Luna Lane's Cable problem wouldn't be so pressing. "Maybe she turned away investigators, too, or made you all forget they'd stopped by."

"Eithne?" Abdel studied me. "The witch who…?"

"Cursed me," I explained. "And she's back."

The bits of Abdel's smooth, golden skin poking through his wrappings grew wan. "What can we do?"

"Nothing." Sighing, I leaned back. I stared up at the gothic-style three-floor manor behind us where the vampires lived. "But I just wanted you to know."

"Surely, there's *something* we can do," said Abdel. "I have to alert the town—"

"No," said Roan quickly. "No, you just sit back, Mr. Mayor. We're getting to the bottom of this."

"And how do you propose to do that?" Abdel asked. "I really do insist you let me help you."

Chione turned the car off and got out, walking around to hold the passenger's side door for her distant relative.

"Well, I could ask you some questions." I stared

at the game in my hand. "And maybe it'd be safe for you to join us in a round of Evidence."

Mayor Abdel smoothed his navy blue suit as he stood, Chione shutting the door behind him.

"A round of…?" he asked.

"Just wait inside." I nodded to the vampire manor. "First I need to check on—"

As if on cue, a howl ripped out into the night sky, followed by one, two, three, and four more howls in unison.

"Oh," said Abdel, nonplussed. "Full moon."

Full moon was right. As fast as I could, I pumped my legs and skidded around the Vadas home, heading for the latched gate.

"Faine?" I cried out. "Everyone all right back there?"

Panting and slobbering filled the air. Good. That meant the kids were probably running around, working off their excess energy.

There was another howl up at the full moon, and suddenly remembering I had nothing to hide at the moment, I jumped up and cast an enchantment. "ETATIVEL." I motioned to my legs, letting the enchantment take me clear over the gate and to the backyard.

No sooner had my ballet slippers touched the dirt than the slobbering, snarling, and panting sounds grew louder, the earth practically shaking at my feet.

I dropped the game to the soil as the smallest

werewolf pup came slamming into my arms, licking my face.

I laughed, the bristly tongue tickling even more than Broomhilde's brush.

"Hey, Falcon. Who's a good pup? Who's a good pup?" I squeezed his gray, fuzzy cheeks between my hands, my lips puckering up for a little puppy nose kiss. He was antsy, his eyes a bit wild, and he accepted my kiss but quickly departed, running around with all the energy of a caged animal finally set free. He pawed at the gate, and his mom nudged him backward, but after that, his sisters—one with curly, brown fur, the other with sleek gray— slammed into me on both sides, and I showered them too with pets and kisses.

A low rumbling filled the air and behind the kids circled the two larger wolves. One brown, one gray, the gray just slightly larger than the brown, the brown's wide, dark eyes always reminding me of the way my best friend looked at me as a human.

"Sorry I'm late," I said to her. "I can't even begin to explain—"

The brown wolf stepped forward, Falcon on her tail, and with a little yip, she nudged her daughters away from my side. Fauna had been standing on the board game beside me, a set of pawprints now decorating the cover.

"Oh!" I said, jumping to my feet and brushing off the dirt. I picked up the game, and the pups looked up at it curiously. "Not for you," I said, to which Falcon and Fauna whined. "It's not a fun game," I explained. Their tails whapped hard against the dirt, hard enough to shoot up little bits of grass and soil.

"NAELC." I gestured to the box in my hand, wincing at the crack of the new scale on my arm as I moved. At least Roan's jacket covered it. Still, Faine's head grew pert, and she sniffed the air at my elbow, getting closer to the scale.

"Yeah," I said. "I messed up—but there are more important things we need to worry about right now."

Faine the wolf whined and nudged my elbow with her nose.

I patted her back, then stared closer at the bottom of the box. The ghoulish cartoons of my mom, of Mrs. Flores, and all the game characters stared back at me—and with lightning clarity, I really, truly recognized Romario Sparklebreath for the first time.

It was Mayor Abdel, minus the wrappings. Surely.

And Mayor Abdel, unlike the other two, was clearly still alive.

So what could the pattern be here? Why those three? Why not anyone else in town?

"Faine, I have to get next door," I explained. "Will you and the family be all right?"

My eyes scanned the backyard. The kids had grown bored waiting for me to hand over the game they couldn't have played just then even if I'd let them, instead chasing their sister and father as they ran after a moth that danced from one backyard torch light to the next.

Faine cocked her head but nodded, nudging at me to head toward the gate.

"I'll come back if I can," I said, unhooking the latch. "I'm sorry—it's such a hectic day."

Faine let out a little yip, standing upright as straight as a statue. They seemed okay.

All right then.

I mussed the top of her head and opened the gate.

If it weren't the full moon, I'd explain everything. But right now, before the county police got here, before Leana and perhaps the others' spirits had to tarry for one night longer… I had to finish this game.

On Draven's front door, there was a cat door—only it was quite high up—on the solid, black-painted wood bound with metal lattice grating. Because rather than a cat door, it was a bat door, of course, decorated with a metal cutout of a bat. If Cable ever stopped by, I'd have to explain that the trio's theme bar extended to their home life. There were people out there obsessed with the gothic aesthetic in towns other than Luna Lane. Right?

I knocked and Qarinah pulled the full-sized door open, a grin flitting on her face. "Dahlia, come in. We've been expecting you."

"Who's watching the pub?" I asked as I stepped inside.

"Ravana and Todd." She offered to take my—or Roan's—coat and I obliged, shifting out of it. She winced. "New scale?"

"Yeah." I rubbed at it subconsciously. The last new scale no longer itched, but this one—this was far too large. It didn't seem fair to jump from a scale the size of a quarter to *this*.

"It seems like there's a lot going on in town, but you can't forget to take care of yourself." She spoke with the soft but firm rebuke of a mother.

Wincing, I gave her a half-shrug. "So people keep reminding me."

"And it looks like you do indeed need reminding."

It wasn't Qarinah who'd spoken, but the smooth, sultry tone that could only belong to Draven. He filed down his staircase, adjusting a cuff-link at his wrist. He was wearing a dark suit jacket, a flowing dress shirt beneath it that spilled out in frilly white cuffs over his wrist. He looked more archaic than usual, but the outfit certainly suited him.

His lips pinched together as he reached the bottom of the steps. "I told you to come speak to me *as soon as the sun set*."

"Something came up."

His gaze traveled up and down my exposed arm. "And that was why you failed to prevent the spread of your stone scales today?"

"Yes," I snapped, covering the new scale defensively. It was so big, a bit of it spilled over between my fingers and I sighed, giving up. "I brought the game."

"So I see." Draven looked over his shoulder, then at Qarinah, before nodding. She slipped away, Roan's jacket over her arm. "Roan explained that Eithne paid you a visit."

"She did."

"And she instructed you to complete the game?"

"She did."

Draven sighed and flung his arms to either side of him. "And you want to... *follow* those instructions?"

I was the fool, huh? "You didn't tell me Eithne was in Luna Lane when Abraham and Jessmyn died."

Draven's face grew grim. "Roan told us it was the Davises. Tragic. Truly."

Right. He hadn't known they were the bones in my backyard. "Eithne," I said, redirecting him to the point at hand.

He swallowed visibly. "The subject never came up."

"The fact that you've known the witch who cursed me, who killed my mother, for *decades* just never came up?"

"I didn't *know* her. Not that well. She kept to herself mostly."

"But you talked to her. You saw her! Did she live in town?"

"Yes." He shrugged. "Well, on the outskirts. In the woods."

"And you've *known this all along*?"

"What do you want me to say?" He flung his arms out to either side. "If I'd told you sooner, you just would have been angry at me all the sooner. We weren't bosom buddies. She lived near town. She performed enchantments—for a price. Prices most weren't willing to pay. She wasn't a very helpful witch, not like you, not like your mother."

I didn't have a response. The anger was simmering beneath my skin.

"I haven't seen her in decades," he said softly. "I swear. Not since… Well, I suppose not since Jessmyn and Abraham moved away."

"Only they didn't move away." I studied Draven's pale complexion. Enchantments were difficult to perform on the undead, but not impossible. Not for a witch of Eithne's caliber. She'd made even him forget. Yet she hadn't wiped his mind of any memories of *her*. He'd just chosen not to share those with me.

Sighing, I decided to let it go. What did it matter? He wasn't my boyfriend anymore anyway. I held the game up and tapped the illustration of

Romario Sparklebreath with one finger. "This is Abdel."

Draven opened his dark red lips, the slight tip of a fang poking out, but he shut his mouth and examined it closer. "That image changed."

"Not since last night," I pointed out.

"No…" Draven rubbed his chin as he stared at the box. "But back in the day, it was different. I'm fairly certain."

"'Fairly certain'? Why didn't you tell me this before?"

"I didn't think about it. I didn't recognize him. And it's been so long, I forgot what the card used to look like."

"Ravana didn't seem to be surprised about Mrs. Flores." I pointed to Dame Sanguine. "And I think she tried to keep my mom's card out of play so Cable wouldn't notice since we looked alike."

"She did." Draven nodded.

"And?"

"And what?"

I smacked my forehead. "Why are Luna Lane residents—past and present—in this cursed game?"

"Cursed? Not enchanted?" he asked.

Did the wording really make a difference? "Eithne admitted to putting magic on it, so I would call it cursed, like anything else she's had a hand in. But she claimed she had nothing to do with Leana's death—or Jessmyn's and Abraham's murders."

The look that crossed Draven's face was unreadable. But I sure didn't like that there wasn't any surprise on there.

"I can't! Dear, I'm not thirsty just now." Qarinah's smooth, soprano tones carried out from the vampires' dining room, lit in the dark only by a candle chandelier and the bright beams of moonlight that filtered in through the three large windows on one side of the room. They overlooked the Vadases' house.

"Dining room," of course, applied quite loosely.

There was a long table and chairs, but there was never any food on this table. Not of the variety the rest of us enjoyed anyway.

At the moment, Chione was lying across it, sprawled out and tugging at her collar to expose her neck.

"Chione, dear, come on now. This is embarrassing." Mayor Abdel tugged at his granddaughter, pulling her down off the table.

Qarinah sent a look to Draven and shrugged, then took a seat beside Roan at the table.

Sometimes, if the vampires weren't careful, the bloodbags could get a *little* unwieldly.

Chione hissed as she slid off the table.

"If you won't feed on me, I see no reason to stay here." She dashed past Draven and me, practically barreling into me. "I know *you* won't take a taste," she said sharply to Draven before she headed for the front door, the slam of the ornate, heavy thing echoing out across the manor.

That was… so entirely unlike Chione. Her grandfather came first. Always. And she'd just left him here?

But then there was the other thing she'd said. "You won't feed on her?" I asked.

Draven put a hand on his hip and offered a bored shrug. "I haven't fed on a woman since… Well, since you."

I raised an eyebrow. "Does male blood taste like steak or something?"

"More like the blood of someone you love makes the rest taste like the rotten decay of filth beneath your feet." His heavily eyeshadowed eyes flitted to the floor.

I squirmed in place. If only Draven had been this romantic when we'd actually stood a chance.

But now I'd never forgive him for keeping quiet about Eithne. Not enough to be more than casual friends anyway.

"Lia? Shall we play the game?" Roan didn't even stir as Qarinah slipped an arm through his, and I filed that casual touch away to ask him more about at another date.

My first instinct was a sharp pang of jealousy on my mother's behalf—when I knew my mother would be *overjoyed* for her good friend to finally move on from the love she could never have returned.

I shook my head to clear it.

The game.

"I told Abdel, Draven, and Qarinah everything you told me," he said. "And they agreed."

Abdel sat down at the head of the table next to Roan and threaded his fingers together. "Most puzzling. Still, if it'll explain these awful things staining the reputation of Luna Lane… Let's play."

I sat down beside him, across from Roan, and Draven seated himself without a word to my left.

I shoved the game, upside down, toward Abdel at first.

He cocked his head slightly but then examined the game.

A wrapping-covered finger stopped over the illustration I'd so recently pinpointed as him.

"How did this game maker know my face?" He patted his facial wrappings subconsciously.

"I don't think this was made by just any game maker." I opened the box and pointed to the illustrated corpse of "Lady E." "Or if it was, it's been warped by Eithne's magic."

I took the character cards and shuffled. "Anyone know where Virginia is?" Perhaps the more players, the more people who'd have the chance to tell everyone about what happened here—whatever was about to happen.

Roan shook his head, looking to Abdel and the vampires in turn. No one claimed to have seen the ghost.

She could be anywhere. Curious about Milton. Flirting with Cable… Off in a huff somewhere, moaning about how she couldn't have fun if people cheated in a game.

"All right then. Let's just say the Luna Lane Games Club has a rotating selection of players."

"More like the Spooky Games Club if you ask me," said Qarinah. Her eyes sparkled and she dug her hand even more into Roan's forearm. "Who wants to play boring old games when you can play a game enchanted by a witch?"

Draven let out a harsh breath as he passed out the game sheets and a pen or pencil from the box— I supposed we'd just gathered all of those up the night before without thinking—to each player. "*Really*, Qarinah?"

She slunk back into her seat somewhat. She wasn't anywhere near as bold as Ravana, her vampire sire.

"Sorry," she said simply.

"Spooky Games Club it is." I shrugged and finished mixing up each pile. "The only thing I'd point out is that it's a *cursed* game. *Enchanted* makes me think the magic was done for good or at least innocuous reasons."

"*That* would arguably be in the eye of the beholder." Draven folded his hands as he sat back down.

I let that slide. Now was not the time.

"Roan, you're not playing," I said, the stack of cards in my hand. "You're human. It's too risky." Without looking at my choices, I slid the three solution cards face down in the "solution" envelope, then passed out the character cards.

"Now hold on a minute," Roan said, taking the card I'd meant for Qarinah and sliding it toward himself. "I'm the lawman here, and I have as much right as you to know what happened and what this game has to do with it. *More* right."

Why could he be so stubborn?

He flipped the card and Qarinah got a good look. "We'll play as a team. How about that?"

I didn't like it. But if Qarinah was the player and Roan was just watching alongside her…

"All right," I acquiesced.

Abdel got himself, more or less. This time, Roan and Qarinah were the boy Darling twin, and Draven was Madame Sanguine. I got my mom.

I straightened my hat, channeling all of the magical energy floating in the air straight down inside me. "Let's play."

Nothing seemed too strange for the first few rounds of play. There wasn't even any thunder this time, and though there were howls whenever the room got too quiet, the vampires knew what their neighbors got up to during the full moon.

Still, in this dark dining room, Qarinah's assessment of us being the town's Spooky Games Club didn't seem far-off.

"This is dull," said Draven as he finished taking his turn. He crossed something out on his game sheet, then tossed his pen down, folding his arms in front of him. "So much for spooky games."

She *had* said to finish the game until completion. And it wasn't like anything odd had happened the last time we'd played.

"Did anything… *untoward* ever happen when you played this game with the first Games Club?" I asked.

"You mean, besides an unending sense of boredom?" Draven flinched as Qarinah giggled and took her turn, conspiring with Roan behind a pale brown hand. Draven scratched his chin. "The last time we played the game before all of this—Ravana and I, I mean—was after Jessmyn and Abraham had moved."

"You mean, after they'd been murdered."

Abdel quietly took his turn, his lips sliding into a frown.

"Yeah, come to think of it, it was the last time we played games with the Woodwards, too."

It was my turn now. I rolled the dice and found myself in the greenhouse illustrated on the game board and unearthed a piece of evidence. On the board tending to the flowers was Frankenstein's monster in gardener's overalls. I crossed myself—Flowery Allspice—off the list of suspects. At least I wasn't going to be doing any sneaking.

I handed the dice to Draven and then did a double-take.

On the board, an illustrated shovel moved. I blinked.

"Wait!" I pointed to the greenhouse. "That shovel—it flipped over."

Abdel was nearest the image and he peered down closely. "I didn't see, but it *is* upside down. The shovel head is upright. Hard to keep a shovel leaning like that."

Roan and Qarinah grew quiet, the latter's lips pursing, but neither had anything to add.

"Perhaps you're seeing things." Draven snatched the dice out of my hands.

"We're playing a cursed game and you accuse me of *seeing* things," I muttered. I kept an eye on the shovel, everyone else's attention diverted.

"As I was saying," said Draven, moving his game piece but not reaching a room to uncover a new clue, "Milton and Leana seemed... out of sorts."

Off in the horizon, one of the kids howled. Their cries were higher in tone than their parents', so it was easy for me at least to tell them apart.

"How so?" I asked.

"I don't know." He passed the dice along. "Distracted. Sad. Leana could barely look any of us in the eye. Milton was particularly prone to snapping, which Ravana found amusing, which in turn irritated Milton all the more. They argued."

"About what?"

Draven's jaw clenched. "Nothing of import," he said quickly—too quickly. He was lying... But why?

"He didn't even want to finish the game. I chalked their moods up to their best friends leaving town all of a sudden just a couple of weeks earlier—"

"But they may have had guilty consciences," added Roan, his brows drawn together as Qarinah took their turn.

I frowned.

The shovel jumped up—caught in its two-dimensional prison, but jumping up nonetheless—and whacked down its broad end over the back of the Frankenstein monster gardener's head.

The creature collapsed to the ground, Xs appearing across its eyes—dead.

Chapter Seventeen

"*H*ey!" I screamed, pointing to the greenhouse.

Everyone looked again. Roan frowned. "Was the gardener always dead?"

"No!" I tapped a finger against him, against the shovel, which now lay beside him, as if I could reach through the board and lift them out into reality.

I waved my hand over the greenhouse, closing my eyes and *feeling* for a ripple in energy.

There was something *familiar* about the energy surging up from beneath my palm, but I couldn't put a name to it.

"Blunt force to the back of the head," said Roan. "In the garden. With a shovel."

My eyes flew open. "Jessmyn and Abraham?" Why was the board showing us this? Eithne? Why tease us like this? "But Eithne claimed they were killed somewhere else…"

She could have been lying, but why bother if she was so amused by my unskilled detective work?

With a moan, a marshmallow-looking cartoon ghost shifted on the game board.

I jumped to my feet. "You see this, right? All of you?"

Abdel backed his chair up, and I wondered how he'd gotten to be so ancient and still afraid of the paranormal. Qarinah nodded mutely, everyone's eyes stuck on the ghost, who grabbed the shovel and dragged it through the illustrated house straight up the little cartoon stairs and ladder and to the attic. The ghost dropped the shovel with a clatter I could actually hear and floated backward, gesturing wildly at the bottom of an illustrated collection of shelves.

"In the attic!" I said. "Jessmyn and Abraham were killed with the shovel in the attic."

The little ghost put its flowy, blobby arms at its sides, as if putting its fists on its hips.

"Whose attic?" asked Qarinah.

The ghost's blobby head transformed into an actual marshmallow.

"Virginia…?" I asked aloud. No. It wasn't possible. Could it be?

With an audible *whoosh*, the ghost headed down the cartoon ladder and to the mansion's bowling alley. It pointed wildly at the round zombie head running down the bowling lane that was supposed to represent a bowling ball.

"We didn't finish," said Draven, snapping me out of my concentration.

"What?" I turned back to him.

"That last game with the Woodwards. They were acting distracted, and Leana jumped up, running upstairs. Milton chased after her, saying we ought to finish. But she wouldn't." His stare grew distant. "Yes, he came back down and said she wasn't feeling well and we'd have to finish another time. But the next few times Ravana and I came back, neither of them would play with us. Ravana seemed rather bored with it all, so I gave up after a while. I found some relief that Leana and he eventually played games together again, but the club... That was the last night Games Club ever met, and we'd already been down two members."

The little ghost picked up the zombie bowling ball and threw it back down, its amorphous arms on its hips.

"The bowling ball?" I ventured. The ghost floated in circles.

Bowling ball. Attic.

There'd been that crusty substance on the bowling ball I'd found in Milton's attic, which I'd wiped on my dress. Later, when I'd gone to clean it...

I realized, with a start, it had been dried blood.

"The shovel... You were just showing someone

getting smacked in the back of the head. They were killed with the bowling ball in the attic?"

The marshmallow ghost got even more excited, zipping around the whole of the cartoon mansion.

"What bowling ball?" asked Roan.

"There was one in the attic," I explained. My toe stung just thinking about it. "Milton's attic. I didn't think much of it, but Ginny was there when I stubbed my toe—*Virginia*."

"Can someone please explain what's going on here?" asked Abdel.

I'd almost forgotten he was playing with us.

"Ginny!" I called out, tracing fingers over the board to try to catch the ghost. *She* was the familiar energy. "Ginny's trapped in the game!"

The room went quiet, the only sound the distant, tinny *whoosh* the ghost made throughout the game.

"How?" Roan asked.

"I don't know," I admitted. Closing my eyes, I spread both palms over the game board, channeling what magical energy I could through my pointed hat. "ESAELER!" I cried out, another piercing howl echoing at the moon. "EMOC, AINIGRIV!"

The board rattled beneath my fingers.

"Keep going," encouraged Draven. "She's shifting."

"EERF AINIGRIV TES!"

With a thunderous *whoosh*, the board shook, the pieces scattering, and I opened my eyes. Virginia's upper torso appeared as if pushing up through the game, her broad hat askew.

"About time you noticed," she said dryly. "What did you think that evil witch meant when she told you you'd bound a friend to aid you in more intimately investigating the game? *Intimate* is right. You gave me a front-row seat." She huffed.

"I... I bound you?" I stepped back.

Virginia heaved herself up and Roan and Abdel quickly swooped in, each taking a corporeal arm to lift her out of there.

"Thank you, gentlemen," she said as her feet reached the ground—or near it, since she usually preferred hovering.

She spun on me. "You trapped me in there!"

"I did?" The accusation stung like a slap. "But... When? How? It had to have been Eithne."

"I was in the game by the time she showed up." Virginia sighed. "I was with you all night before that! Didn't you notice me?" She looked at both Draven and me.

We exchanged a look and both shook our heads.

Virginia put her hands on her hips and stomped her foot. "That red ectoplasm. Had to be. Took away your powers, made it so you couldn't see me. I thought you were both just being *rude* as usual when you were ignoring me. I backed off, gave you some space to concentrate." She shrugged. "But I was there all night. Arrived right before Faine. I had to fly around and let some of my irritation at the rampant *cheating* wear off first. But I flew in and you two were..." She stared pointedly at Draven. He didn't flinch. "Anyway, ask her if you don't believe me. We talked to each other on the way over. At least *she's* always polite," she muttered.

I couldn't ask Faine anything just now.

"That's ridiculous," I said. "The red ectoplasm didn't affect Draven at all. Besides, you don't have to be paranormal to see you." I gestured at Roan, who was looking right at Virginia, the bags under his eyes really popping in the dim candlelight.

"No, but maybe you have to be away from that warped goo."

"You were there when I found it——"

"And you accused me of getting paler, right? That probably explains that. Maybe the longer you're around it, the more it sets in."

"Okay." I had no reason to disbelieve her. "But how did I——"

"Trap me?" She crossed her arms. "As soon as Draven flew away with the stuff, I opened my mouth and got half a word out before you shouted, "BIND!" backward, swinging your hand my way, and *poof*, there I went straight into the game. You didn't even see me *then*?"

Everyone stared at me and I winced. "I was trying an idea that popped in my head. Thought I'd bind any energy surrounding the game straight into it, that maybe that would be key to revealing the curse at the core of it." I shrugged. "I thought it didn't work."

"Well, it did." Virginia huffed and took a seat at a plush, high-back chair behind the table beside one of the large windows. "And I had nothing much to *do* in there besides search for any clues for you. Might not have bothered if I'd known you'd be so ungrateful, except it wasn't just *for you.*"

It was my turn to huff a little. "Of course I'm grateful. Just… How did you figure that out? About the bowling ball and the attic?"

"Oh." Virginia grew stiff. "So there wasn't much *inside* the world of the game, so to speak. No one else moving around. But oh, it was noisy, like you know how you're in a crowded room and the conversations around you sound like bees a-buzzing? Like that. Lots of talking, nothing distinct. Gave me quite a headache, I was sure, even though I haven't had a headache since I was living. So it was getting to be too much and I was lying back on the *fainting couch*"—she gestured to the drawing of a red divan in the cartoon living room—and I looked up. Just now, anytime I looked up, I saw the lot of you, staring down, rolling thunderous dice atop the invisible roof of the place. But when the game box was closed, you know what I saw? *Us.* Playing the game last night."

"I don't understand." Draven crossed his arms, his eyes narrowing suspiciously.

"Well, *you* try being shut up in a noisy game for

more hours than you can count and see how much *you* understand. All I can tell you is after that whole display, I saw elderly Milton and elderly Leana playing it by themselves for a very short round, rather grim looks on their faces. They didn't seem to be having fun. After that, I saw *you* playing it. You and Ravana dressed like Sonny and Cher or something, along with a much younger-looking Milton and Leana."

Sonny and Cher? I wondered at times where this hundred-year-old ghost got her references.

"You didn't finish the game," she explained, which corroborated Draven's story. "Milton seemed rather cross with you. He walked out before the game could end. But I couldn't hear what was said —not over that *noise*. But you also left out an important detail when describing that final game to Miss Poplar just now. That's right, I could hear *you all* now just fine. Once you took the game box top off, it grew rather quiet until the dice started that thundering sound." She fluffed at her bun. "In that game decades back, Milton was fixated on a couple of character cards, pointing and waving them in your and Ravana's faces. It wasn't until later when I had more of the full picture that I noticed they didn't look the same in the first few games."

Draven grimaced, an incisor biting his lower lip. "We noticed," he said. "Long before that day, even. Mrs. Flores—the character card had changed to look like her. Then the Sparklebreath card changed.

He used to be blond. We just didn't recognize *you* then." He nodded at Abdel.

So Draven had been only "fairly certain" the card had changed, huh? And now he was saying he remembered noticing right way? What else was the vampire keeping from me?

Abdel held his hands up. "I had nothing to do with that, I swear. I've never even *seen* this game before tonight. I was friendly with Milton and Leana, with Jessmyn and Abraham, too, but the only one of them I'd even consider a friend was Abraham." His eyes grew soft. "When he worked at town hall, he did discuss leaving to run for state legislature in a more populous part of the state." He slipped his wrapped hands into his suit jacket pocket. "I never really questioned him moving away, considering how often he told me how much he admired me and wanted to get into politics, too." He shook his head softly.

"Why'd you keep that from us?" I asked Draven. "About the cards?"

"I didn't *keep it* from you." He looked sullen, his lips growing pouty. "Ravana and I both told you Mrs. Flores's card wasn't like that originally." He just hadn't told me that Sparklebreath had changed, too. I sighed.

Roan scratched his bearded cheek. "Hey, do you remember Mrs. Flores? She had dementia, too, those last few years—she often spoke about Jessmyn. Never met the woman, but Mrs. Flores always acted as if she'd just seen her that afternoon. 'Jessmyn brought me a pie,' she'd say, and she'd point to a loaf of bread or the like. 'Jessmyn asked me to teach her to cross stich.' I figured she was just confused."

I hoped in Mrs. Flores' case that was just her warped memory, and not a literal sign of Jessmyn's spirit hanging around her all these years without the rest of us noticing.

"Jessmyn and Mrs. Flores were close," said Draven. "Mrs. Flores wasn't always like you remember her." He nodded to Roan and me. "She was a regular queen bee in Luna Lane once. Won every festival ribbon she could, had the best recipes, the most gorgeous craft projects—"

"And Jessmyn, when she lived here, was right there behind her," added Abdel. "Always second place." He smiled wistfully at memories that probably didn't seem so long ago in the span of his long life. "But there was no bad blood between them. In fact, Jessmyn looked up to her. Like the mother she'd never had, I think Abraham once told me. She admired her."

The house went quiet again.

"That's the second time you've said that," I said. "About the Davises *admiring* people."

Roan cocked his head. "What are you thinking?"

I stepped to the game board, only slightly mussed despite Virginia's movements, and picked up the Sparklebreath and Sanguine cards. "Abraham and Jessmyn *admired* Mayor Abdel and Mrs. Flores and after they disappeared, the character cards changed to reflect the people they most admired? That can't be coincidence."

"Those cards changed before then," said Draven. His eyebrows scrunched together. "I'm sure of it. We'd play, we'd pack it away, and then the next time we played, a card might have changed. Though it only happened twice back then. We all discussed what the changes could mean. None of us figured out the 'most admired' person, though. Abraham himself didn't even recognize Abdel, thanks to those wrappings he always has on!"

So they didn't change after they died? Was my theory totally wrong then?

Roan stared at the card that resembled my mom. "Then Cinnamon…?"

"She didn't appear until we played recently." I confirmed my observation silently with Draven, who nodded. But then again, he hadn't played the game since the seventies before yesterday, so how would he know? "Perhaps because of Leana…?" Why not? The other two cards corresponded to the other two people who'd been murdered. "Whom did she most admire?" I looked to Roan to confirm the information that would at least hold up the "most admired" theory.

He tucked his hands into his belt and nodded slowly. "Well, sure, I'd say Leana and Cinnamon got along great. She was Cinnamon's best friend."

"Other than you," I pointed out. His face grew flush at the compliment. "But maybe in Leana's eyes, my mom was the person she admired most. She took her death hard."

"Your mother did do this town a lot of good," said Mayor Abdel softly.

So now I had a partial theory to explain the character cards. The question was, *when* had these cards changed? If Draven was right and at least two cards had changed before the Davises had disappeared, did the magic even relate to their souls being lost? How could it not, though?

Virginia cleared her throat. "If you're all finished now, can I please finish explaining how I uncovered the truth?"

Everyone in the room turned to her. She straightened and crossed her ankles, resting her hands atop her knee. "After the game with the vampires, I saw another game being played— Milton, Leana, and two people I'd identify as Jessmyn and Abraham." She paused for emphasis, positively reveling in what she was about to say next. "They actually didn't even start playing, just set the game up, the tension in the air so thick, you could cut it with a knife. Then the tension burst and everyone was arguing, though it was like a silent picture to me. They all kept looking off, too, every so often, their mouths closing as they stared in one direction—but then they'd start in on each other again."

"One direction?" I asked. "What were they looking at when they went quiet?"

She shrugged. "Something in the kitchen maybe? I don't know. I could only see what the open game board would show me. Finally, the arguing got so bad, Milton snatched the game board and its pieces and shoved them in the box all wrong. I could still see out of half the game left uncovered. He ran upstairs with the game box still open, the pieces scattering and trailing down behind him. Almost made me nauseous, let me tell you, if I *could* feel nauseous again. The game tucked under one arm, he climbed up into the attic, the angry Davises following him—that's what I saw then. Their crazed, even *murderous* faces. And when he turned around, the game box now clutched to his chest, Leana slowly made her way up the ladder with a bowling ball under her arm. Milton cried out and before the Davises could react, Leana's hands were over her head clutching that bowling ball, and she brought it down over the back of Jessmyn's skull."

Leana?

Almost as if in empathy with the victim, the edges of my vision went black.

Chapter Eighteen

"Milton cried out," Virginia continued. "Abraham seemed to scream and he fell to his knees, clutching his wife's body—and then Leana clocked him on the head, too." She *tsked*. "Milton dropped the game box then, and I didn't see any more. After that, there were scenes of more boring games. Nothing much happened, everyone seemed to be having a good time, and eventually the images died out entirely."

My knees growing weak, I grabbed the edge of the dining room table. Leana had killed her neighbors? Milton was covering for her? The latter made sense, at least... And I was glad to know Milton hadn't harmed them. But he'd covered it up and besides...

Leana, one of my mom's best friends, the woman so like my grandmother. No. She couldn't have been capable of such a thing, either.

Everyone else moved slowly to take their seats again, as if at a loss of anything else to say or do.

"I could shift the focus of the investigation to Leana," said Roan after a beat. "Give Milton a break. But if he knew and helped her hide the bodies…"

Milton was doomed either way.

"He wouldn't want you to do that," I said softly. "And I don't believe, not for one second, that Leana was a cold-blooded killer."

A deeper howl echoed out and punctured the room. Grady, most likely.

"Virginia," I said. "Before the-the *murders*. What else was odd about the game that night? Why did Milton run off with the game box up to the attic? Why the bowling ball?"

Virginia tilted her head, tapping a single finger against her knee. "Well, the whole lot of them were in a foul mood, I'd say. I couldn't tell you what they were discussing—only the conversation during the game you played just now was clear as day to me— but they all looked… tired. Exhausted, even. And the bowling ball is easy enough to explain. There were five of them in bags by the couch beside the game table. Abraham was even wearing a bowling shirt."

"Exhausted?" asked Draven, stiffening.

But I was caught on something else she'd said. Five balls? Not four…?

"Their faces were, like, *drained*," Virginia

explained. "Purple bags under their eyes. Their posture kind of droopy. In the games that took place before that, which I watched after, they all looked like they were having fun."

"What about the character cards?" I asked, desperate to find the connection. "If they changed while Jessmyn and Abraham were still playing…"

Virginia looked thoughtful a moment. "I did notice a few of the characters looked different in those earlier games. From my perspective, they were like cartoon characters moving all around me—let me tell you, that is something you do *not* want to experience. Made me question if I ever even really existed." She huffed, staring me down. "But as for why they changed, I couldn't say for sure. I couldn't hear what anyone was saying when they played in those previous games. I suppose… I suppose there was a couple of games where someone would deal out the cards and point animatedly at one of them. Yes, that was it. But everyone just laughed. They seemed to find the changes amusing."

Hmm. That didn't make sense at all. Who'd find a cursed game *amusing*?

"Even Draven laughed!" Virginia added excitedly. "I don't think I've ever *seen* him laugh."

Draven clutched the edge of the table but didn't otherwise respond. "The games that came right before the Davises died," he said grimly. "You said they were having fun. But did they seem… fatigued?"

What was he getting at?

Qarinah let out a little yelp, and I stared at her. She squeezed Roan's arm, and my attention diverted to him. To those purple bags under his eyes, his haggard, *exhausted* appearance. My mouth gaped open.

Virginia tilted her head. "I suppose so. Compared to those earlier games. The four or so games right before that murderous night—I guess the three of them were getting a bit tired."

"Three?" I asked, the gears whirring in my head.

"Jessmyn, Abraham, and Leana." She nodded. "Milton never looked so out of it as the rest of them. And neither did Draven or Ravana, of course. Ravana always looked downright *giddy*, like she was having just an *amazing* time. I remember Abraham practically *threw himself* at her one game to Ravana's delight and his wife didn't even care! She just scooted closer to Ravana, practically getting into a fight with Leana to sit on the other side of her."

"And what did Draven do?" I turned to ask the vampire himself.

Draven jumped up from his seat without a word, turned into a bat, and floated toward the front door, right out through the hatch at the top of it.

"Draven!" I shouted, but he was gone.

"Now what could have gotten *him* so worked up?" Virginia asked. "Draven wasn't there that time everyone was throwing themselves at Ravana. He didn't always show when she did. Though he never came without her, either." She shrugged.

"What am I missing?" asked Abdel.

I turned on Qarinah. "Did the original Games Club ever donate blood?"

She looked taken aback. "That was before I turned, darling. I couldn't say what Ravana and Draven got up to back then. I wasn't here."

Abdel answered for her. "Sure, they did, I guess. Pretty much everyone in town did their part to keep our children of the night fed." He shrugged. "No one minded helping out."

Roan groaned and cradled his head. Qarinah swooped in to ask him what was wrong.

"Except Milton," Abdel added. "I remembered he got quite squeamish about it. The people in town then used to tease him. Suppose Milton got the last laugh. He's the last of the humans from those days left." He chuckled. "Maybe there was something to be said for the vampire-venom-free diet."

That did seem odd. What had become of them all? Luna Lane was a nice, quiet town, perfect for retirement. And we took care of our elderly. I couldn't see every single one of them moving to greener pastures when they hit old age. What was greener than Luna Lane?

Was it all a coincidence?

Where were the elderly people in Luna Lane?

"Roan, what's wrong?" I asked, seeing as he looked about to be sick.

"Nothing." He waved me off. "Just tired is all."

"Roan, have you been letting both Draven and Ravana feed on you as well?" Qarinah narrowed her eyes at the sheriff. So he let *her* feed on him, that wasn't up for debate.

"Just Ravana." He scratched his neck. "Draven doesn't drink much, but Ravana..." He shook his head. "She's rough with it."

"Ravana has a thirst like a woman parched in the desert," said Abdel. "She's been feeding off Chione the past couple of days. I really can't stand for any excess that might impede work performance. I was going to talk to her about it tonight, but we came upon the sheriff and got distracted."

"Chione's addicted," said Qarinah. She gulped as all our eyes turned on her. "I didn't know until I saw her tonight, prostrating herself like that. But an addicted bloodbag can be dangerous. It's just one step away from going blood mad." She winced. "I didn't want to get Ravana in trouble. I'm sure she wouldn't push it too far—she's my sire," she added quietly.

Roan patted her lap and Qarinah offered him a flattering smile.

"But I won't let her feed on you anymore, my sheriff."

"I don't mind being a one-gal bloodbag." He smiled back.

Now was not the time to marvel at this romance before me, though.

A series of howls rang out in the night now, followed by what could only be described as a crash, a thunderous clatter of something like logs falling.

"What was that?" The bits of Mayor Abdel's skin that peeked through the white cloth looked almost as washed out as his wrappings.

Somehow, I knew at once. I ran to the window. The fence leading to the Vadases' backyard was smashed—the gate hanging on by a hinge and several jagged pieces of wood, the rest scattered along the grass and off to the sidewalk.

"The werewolves!" I shouted.

I should never have left them to play a game, no matter how important.

My best friend and her family only really, truly needed me once a month, and I'd let them down.

My skin itched. Just like I'd let this town down time and again.

But why now? Why tonight? They usually had a handle on it. I was just there for backup, in case something like this happened...

I spun on Qarinah. "Where did Draven go in such a hurry?"

Obviously, something was wrong when he'd left, but I'd been in the middle of so many revelations, I couldn't think straight.

Qarinah shirked at my approach. "I don't know. Not for certain," she added quieter.

"Then you have a guess!"

Roan put a hand on Qarinah's shoulder. "Lia, calm down. Don't bite the messenger—"

I growled at him. It actually sounded animal-like.

"He left when Ginny described the state of the Davises and Leana during the game sessions leading up to that fateful night," I said, a light-bulb going off in my head. "What if... What if they were blood mad? If Chione has a venom addiction, that seems similar to how they acted."

"He *left* when Virginia mentioned them throwing themselves at Ravana," Qarinah corrected.

Of course.

"Dahlia?" said Virginia, hovering in front of me. "What is it? What did you figure out?"

My expression must have been easy to read.

The purple bags under Chione's and Roan's eyes—and Falcon's.

Virginia's account that the Davises and Leana had appeared *exhausted* during the night of the Davises' murder.

Draven's odd behavior the night Leana's body had been taken away.

"Draven and Ravana were part of the original Games Club," I said. "They may not have been able to enchant the game, but... They could have driven humans to murder."

My heartbeat soared upward, clamping down on my throat.

I'd dated a murderer.

Chapter Nineteen

Qarinah's eyes were wide, glossy. "No. We don't drink to excess. The minute someone shows sign of venom addiction, we give them time to recover before we ever consider drinking from them again. *If* we ever drink from them again. If we don't, we could wind up turning them—or worse."

"Worse?" asked Roan. He actually blanched.

"Blood madness," Qarinah whispered. "The state in which humans are blind with fatigue, with rage. They'll do whatever their vampire sires ask of them, desperate for more, for the chance to turn once and for all." Her hands went to her throat. "I've never experienced it myself. Ravana was careful. She gave me just the right amount to turn me, skipping over that step entirely."

"Outrageous!" said Mayor Abdel, straightening

his suitcoat. "The vampires know they're not welcome in this town if they turn *anyone* from Luna Lane. I can't run a harmonious paranormal-and-human town if all the humans become paranormal."

"Which might be why their victims went blood mad," I ventured. "Because you'd notice a new vampire among the town's citizens and banish Draven and Ravana." I thought about it some more. "So they'd have to make sure no one ever got enough vampire venom to turn, but if their appetites were out of control, there'd be a lot of addiction, a lot of blood madness in town."

"And you think we wouldn't notice *that*?" Mayor Abdel scoffed. "They had plenty to drink without resorting to creating blood addiction."

"Plenty to drink isn't the same as being fully satiated," Qarinah said softly.

Abdel blustered. "But then—But then... We'd have *noticed*," he repeated.

A thought struck me. "Not if they all died," I whispered. "Or supposedly moved away." Eithne had helped cover up those two murders. How many more citizens had been drunk dry? "Where's everyone from Milton's generation?" I asked.

"Passed away or moved years ago," said Abdel. "We're a small town. It's not like there were that many of them. It didn't seem strange if..." He went quiet. "We've *never* had a murder in Luna Lane."

Roan scratched his jaw. "That we knew of, mayor. That we knew of. The past two days have proven otherwise."

Mayor Abdel looked about to say something more but stopped himself. Then his eyes went dull. "Chione…"

He ran for the door, not bothering to shut it behind him.

"The kids!" I shouted, panic hitting me like a lightning bolt. If Ravana had made Falcon blood mad—Falcon, a *toddler*, a *werewolf*—he'd be out of control.

"Wait!" shouted Roan from behind me as I headed for the door. "Didn't that evil witch tell you you had to play the game all the way through?"

I turned on my heel, chewing my bottom lip as my gaze darted between Qarinah, Roan, and Virginia and down the walk-up to the sidewalk. A litany of howls pierced the night sky.

"The werewolves first," I said. "Besides, we can't finish the game without Abdel and Draven."

And if I figured out we *had* to finish this game to put Leana's and the Davises' souls to rest, then I would *make* Draven finish playing, even if I had to enchant him—right before he got locked up in jail in Milton's place.

I didn't wait for a response. I was halfway down the sidewalk, following the howls, the bits of damage here and there—a gushing fire hydrant, a trampled bush, a stop sign bent sideways—when a little shriek growing louder and louder behind me caught my attention.

I whirled around to find Broomie soaring above the sidewalk, Goldie clutching for dear life to the top of her shaft, her legs wrapped like pretzels just above her brush.

Goldie's hair was wild, bits and pieces strewn out from her usually carefully made bun.

"Help me!" she cried, her voice as wobbly as someone shouting on a roller coaster.

"POTS!" I shouted to Broomhilde, both my hands out.

She screeched to a halt, poor Goldie flipping around upside down.

"ETATIVEL," I said quietly, aiming the enchantment at Goldie. She must have felt my invisible grip on her because slowly, ever-so-slowly, she let go, one finger at a time. I righted her up and set her down gently on her feet.

Broomie flung straight into my hand. I lost control of Goldie for the last two inches just to catch her.

Goldie grunted but seemed all right.

"What is going on?" I stared at Broomie.

Another howl echoed out in the air—far closer this time.

"I don't know," Goldie said. "She suddenly scooped me up, rammed the door open, and took me flying down the sidewalk at the speed of light."

Her breaths were shallow. "I thought I would fall or the shock would kill me."

Cowed, Broomie slid out of my hand and nudged Goldie with her bristles apologetically.

"It's all right, girl." She patted her back, then she looked at me, aghast. "What's happened? Broomie must have wanted to come help. It was all the howling, I think."

"I can't explain, not right now." I held out my hand for Broomhilde and her shaft flew right into it. "But she needn't have brought you here. Stay back and stay safe." I mounted Broomhilde, my grip the perfect balance of security and control.

"But, Dahlia, perhaps Broomie knows what I've been telling you, that it's all right for *you* to ask others for help—"

But I didn't have time to listen. Broomie and I launched into the air, far, far higher than she'd taken Goldie, and looked down on downtown Luna Lane from above.

My gaze followed the trail of destruction.

It led to the sheriff's office—the front door busted off its hinge almost as badly as the Vadases' gate had been.

And down the sidewalk several blocks over was a peculiar sight.

An old man riding a small werewolf down the concrete, laughing like he was having the time of his life.

A block behind him was Cable, running rather too slowly after his uncle.

So much for keeping the secret of Luna Lane. Unless he was going to buy that a renegade wolf pup had busted his uncle out of jail.

To Milton's right flank, in the road, were four other werewolves: two small, two large, two brown, two gray.

That meant little Falcon was the kidnapper.

I squeezed my knees together and pointed Broomie's handle at the werewolf parade. "There!" I shouted.

We dove.

The air whapped like in the wake of a rocket takeoff against my cheeks. We nearly crashed right into the street, but with a gentle nudge of my ankle, we skirted up just in time, floating between Grady and Faine.

"What's happened?" I asked them, shouting over the force of the air as we all sped after the little renegade.

Faine howled and shook her head really fast. Grady kept his eye on the prize. I supposed the time for discussion was later, when they could actually speak.

But just as Falcon made a sharp turn down a narrow alley, the girls, trailing behind their parents, came to a sudden stop.

I did the same, torn between soaring after Falcon and figuring out what was wrong now.

Faine yelped, and Grady nodded, continuing the chase while Faine circled back to her daughters.

Fauna and Flora growled, bearing their fangs as a figure approached. A flickering streetlight kept the person in shadow, so I flung one of my arms out. "XIF!" The streetlight flickered back to full power.

Cable reached the edge of our block and bent over, his breathing labored as he clutched his knees.

It was just Cable catching up.

The girls' growls grew more guttural, drool dripping from Flora's maw.

Faine leaped between her daughters and the sight of the approaching professor, yipping at the girls sternly.

Cable let out a giant gasp, and I realized—the kids weren't so used to controlling their urges as wolves yet. They didn't need to have become addicted to vampire venom to be dangerous. At least around a simple human who had no idea how to act around werewolves if he wanted to keep his skin on his bones.

And right now—the labored breathing, the sudden stiffness, the backing up—he was acting like prey.

"No!" I shouted as the two girls broke ranks and went either way around their mom, barreling after Cable. Cable ran—faster than he had been before, his survival instincts clearly kicking into gear—but it wouldn't be sustainable, and it wouldn't be fast enough.

"Broomie!" I didn't need to ask her twice.

We barreled after the girls and despite our speed, I managed to lift one arm off Broomhilde, the pressure of the air nearly insurmountable. "POTS!"

But they were too fast, my arm too shaky for the enchantment to connect.

"WOLS!" I screamed, just as Faine managed to catch up with us, the enchantment hitting her instead of either of her girls.

Bananaberries! She was slower now, far too slow to be of help.

Gripping Broomie's handle tighter, I leaned flat against her, increasing our velocity until we whipped past the girls and headed straight for Cable.

He looked over his shoulder, his pace faltering, clearly favoring one leg over the other. His eyes widened, but he couldn't say anything as my hand reached out for him. "EMOC!" I said, and the enchantment took hold of him, lifting him up into the air.

"ETATIVEL!" I said this time, seizing control of him as his limbs flailed helplessly against nothing.

I flipped him over to sit on Broomie behind me, then let him go.

He let out a little cry as if about to lose his balance and then gripped my waist—hard. I choked as we flew up, out of the range of the wolves' jaws. The girls would not be stopped, both leaping after us with a yowl. Flora's maw just barely missed Cable's foot as we ascended higher above Luna Lane.

Broomie held position high above them, allowing me to get my bearings.

"Hurting... Me..." I just barely managed to squeeze the words out between my lips.

"Oh! Sorry!" Cable loosened his grip, but he didn't let go. His hands shook against my abdomen, his chiseled chin flat against my neck as the brim of my hat crushed up against him.

He smelled of old books, of a tea tree oil deodorant or aftershave.

My heartbeat grew steadier as I felt his warm, burly arms gripped against me.

"What... What was that?" he asked between breaths. One hand left my abdomen to touch Broomie's shaft, then quickly returned to anchor against me. "I'm flying! We're *flying*!"

The girls kept leaping up below us, but they didn't have a hope of reaching us. Faine caught up, her pace cut by half, and yipped threateningly at the girls until they stopped leaping entirely, their heads bent low, their tails curled against them.

I pointed one hand at Faine. "ESAELER TNEMTNAHCNE," I said, removing the slowness magic I'd accidentally unleashed on her.

Cable was muttering something under his breath, something resembling a prayer.

"Just another day in Luna Lane," I said by way of answer, kicking at Broomie's bristles. We sped off again, Cable's scream echoing out into the night.

Chapter Twenty

"*P*lease. Too. Fast!" shouted Cable.

"Hang on!" was all I told him. Broomie and I headed straight for where we'd lost Falcon and Milton, soaring down through the alley, brushing through it so fast, we blew some cardboard stacked inside a dumpster clear out of the bin.

If I remembered, I'd pick that up later.

No do-gooder went about littering.

"Dahlia, please!" choked out Cable. "Drop me off!"

"And let the girls catch your scent again? No way!" We banked right sharply and Cable squeezed harder, his cheek flat against my hat and the back of my head.

"All right!" he said. "All right! I knew all along, okay? Mom told me! And I've been here before! I saw you were trying to hide your magic from me and I... I was teasing you! I'm sorry!"

A bent newspaper dispenser. We banked hard left, down another dark alley.

"You knew?" I shouted over the wind. "You *knew*? All along?"

"Yes!" shouted Cable. "And I'm sorry. I saw you floating above the stepstool that first day and I thought... I thought, 'Well, my memories weren't fantasies. Holy smokes, magic is real!' But then you just... You kept trying to hide it all from me." He was babbling now as we made another sharp turn. "I wrote those notes and left my notepad, thinking you'd think I was putting it all together, but I knew! Mom knew I was going to spend a few months here, so she sat me down and prepared me, reminded me of those things I'd tried to forget."

We came to a sudden, crashing halt at a pile of broken glass. It glistened in the moonlight, and from it led a trail of blood.

Inside the old, abandoned bowling alley.

Cable was slow to pick up on what I saw, his heart beating so hard, I could feel it against my back. "I was here as a kid once. I knew about the mummy mayor and the witches next door. You played with me, Dahlia! You did a few magic tricks. I just never saw... Never saw anything like tonight."

"I... I played with you?" I never remembered him coming at all. My head was full of Leana and Milton mentioning "Craigle," talking about future visits.

But I never remembered...

Like dawn coming over the horizon, a memory flashed through my mind.

"Vampires live here." *I tossed my braided pigtail over my shoulder, readjusting my witch's hat. It was too big for me at such a young age.*

Hitesh and Zashil, Goldie and Arjun's sons, let out a spooky "Whoooo!" Hitesh was a year older than his brother, though Zashil towered over him. Other than that, they both had Goldie's straight nose and their dad's puffy cheeks. They could have been twins.

"Stop that, you three!" said Faine. Her brown hair was short, her threadbare purple T-shirt and green shorts her favorite outfit she never wanted to change out of. Unless her mom made her wash it. "He's scared!"

Behind her trembled a portly little fellow with dark hair and glasses.

"But I'm not lying!" I said rather snootily. "Craigle, if you want to spend time in Luna Lane, you have to know these things."

"It's-It's Cab—" started little Cable.

"Broomie!" I called, and from above, my broom zoomed straight for my hands. She was half the size she was now, just right for a child rider. Between her bristles, she chomped on a cornhusk.

Cable let out a shriek and ran down the street.

"That wasn't very kind." Virginia floated down beside me. She must have been hanging around, observing like she always did. She looked so beautiful, so grown-up when I'd been ten.

"I just wanted him to see," I said bitterly, stroking Broomie's bristles. *"He didn't even stay to see the vampires."*

The sun finished setting on the horizon and the door to Draven's manor opened with a lingering creak.

Ravana bared her fangs. "What is this? Little bloodbags come to feed me?" She licked her lips. "Young, fresh blood is so, so sweet."

Hitesh and Zashil looked at one another and then screamed, running down the sidewalk after Cable.

Faine and I exchanged a glance.

Ravana's eyes sparkled as she looked at us, a hand on one hip. "Come here, my sweets."

We didn't scream, but we ran, Broomie picking us both up after a few steps, much to Faine's terror, and flying us out of there.

Ravana's laughter echoed out behind us.

I scratched my scaled forearm. How could I have forgotten?

But that didn't matter.

It was just one less thing to worry about.

I jumped down off of Broomie, my feet crackling against the glass.

Cable seemed suddenly aware of where were, his gaze traveling rapidly over the shattered glass, the streaks of blood.

"Broomie, take him home," I said.

"No." Cable quickly jumped off and landed beside me with a *crunch*, suddenly very in control of his surroundings.

"I thought you were afraid of vampires," I said.

He quirked an eyebrow at me. "You do remember me."

"Sure do, *Craigle*." I nudged him with my elbow for good measure.

Cable stared up at Broomie, flying above us. "I never saw a vampire back then. If I recall, I was more afraid of your broomstick."

I laughed.

Broomie, indignant, shook, positively huffing.

"She's a sweetheart." I patted her brush.

Cable hesitatingly did the same. Broomie moved into his touch, relaxing as he scratched what I imagined might be something like her chin.

"She likes you," I said simply, moving toward the shattered window. "YDIT." I waved my arms, and the glass shifted out of the way, no more dangerous shards of it sticking out from the frame. It collected into a nice pile in the corner.

"Vampires?" Cable prodded, two steps behind me.

"I think Ravana and Draven are behind Falcon acting erratically." I lifted a leg to fit through the empty window frame.

"Falcon… Faine's kid. The little wolf that came in and swept Milton away."

"Right. The Vadas family are werewolves. They turn into wolves on the night of the full moon. They're usually confined to their backyard and don't cause any trouble."

"I don't know if I'd call busting my uncle out of

jail *trouble*." Cable leaped down beside me inside the dark, decrepit bowling alley entryway. "I was about to do the same myself."

"Hmm…" was all I said at first. "You didn't think Milton did it? Despite what he knew?"

"Kill anyone?" he asked. "No, never."

Broomie floated inside beside me and nestled into my hand.

I had a lot to explain to him yet, but there was one thing I could say. "He didn't. Leana killed the Davises, but she wasn't in control of herself. She was addicted to vampire venom." A little critter scurried up ahead in the dark and I froze. "Milton helped her cover it up."

"And Leana?" Cable asked, his voice a whisper. "Did she… Did she die naturally?"

I still hadn't figured that out.

Our feet left carpet, hitting the smooth surface of the lanes. A ragged breathing and slurping sound echoed out from ahead, along with a very human whimper.

"Stop! Stop, son!" Milton.

"WOLG," I said quietly. The fingers on my free hand began to glow.

Milton walked back and forth at the edge of a lane, his foot hitting a pin and sending it flying with a cloud of dust.

In front of him was a pile of fur. Brown and gray, the gray bobbing.

"Stop!" screamed Milton, clutching at the fine wisps of his hair.

"Oh my…" My heart practically stopped.

Before me, the little wolf was munching on a furry leg. A streak of blood ran down the lane to the pile of gray fur I'd seen earlier.

Grady. Passed out… or dead.

His blood dripping from his little son's maw.

Chapter Twenty-One

"*N*o!" I shouted, practically slipping as my ballet flats grew slick with blood across the hard alley floor. I dove for Grady's limp form, and the lights on my fingers flickered out.

I didn't have time to worry about it.

I inspected Grady. He was breathing, his chest rising and falling.

His tongue flopped out of his mouth across sharp canine teeth.

"Grady!" I said. I reached both hands toward him. "LAEH!" I said.

But nothing happened.

I whipped around. Falcon still had his father's foreleg. He was gnawing at it, hair sticking out from between his teeth.

"POTS!" I shouted at him.

Nothing.

Broomie tittered some distance beside me,

circling around Grady sadly. But she stopped suddenly, shaking, as if encountering a force field— or something she didn't like.

What was going on?

"Milton," said Cable. He approached his uncle and the growling little wolf slowly, carefully.

Falcon kept an eye trained on him but kept chewing.

"Cable, be careful!" I shouted. "Milton, come over here. Walk. Walk normally." I didn't want him to raise Falcon's predator instincts any more than they had been.

I patted Grady's head. "I'll stop him," I said. "And then I'll help." My mouth went dry. I couldn't help without my magic.

Without my magic.

I'd been able to use magic at Draven's house, despite the fact that I'd asked him to store the red ectoplasm there. So it probably hadn't been there at all.

Foolish, foolish Dahlia. Pay attention to these things!

Milton shuffled closer toward me. "Leana?" he asked.

"Come on, Milton," I said, not correcting him. "Walk slowly…"

Cable took a few steps to meet his uncle halfway and Falcon yowled, dropping the leg and growling.

"Stop!" I said to Cable, holding out a hand. "GEL, EMOC," I tried on the mangled wolf leg.

Maybe I was wrong about the red ectoplasm being here.

Nothing happened.

A cold, echoing laugh rang out around the empty alleyway, followed by the heavy, slow roll of a bowling ball. "You are *slow* to catch on sometimes, my dear."

I whirled around to the sound of the voice just beyond Grady's limp form.

My eyes adjusting to the darkness, I blinked, but I already knew what I'd find.

Ravana leaned against the ball return of the next lane, one ankle crossed over the other, her arms tucked tightly against her broad chest.

"Ravana! Where's Draven?" I looked around.

"Around." She shrugged and stood straighter, jingling something that glistened red even in the dark in one hand. "Progeny can't disobey their sires, you know. Oh, and thank you for this. So helpful of you to send him home with it last night."

The red ectoplasm. The strange goo that took my powers away.

What a fool I'd been. I'd figured out Draven and Ravana were behind this, and yet... Yet I'd totally forgotten about how I'd handed Draven my weakness on a platter!

Broomie shuddered beside me, and I stepped back to take hold of her, gripping her with both hands to keep my knees from buckling.

"You... What are you doing?" I gestured to

Falcon, who'd gone back to munching. "Drinking from a *toddler*? Making him blood mad—and Chione?" I looked around but didn't see Abdel or Chione anywhere.

"And Roan, too, if my pretty little progeny hadn't latched on to him so deeply." Ravana let a soft breath out between her lips. As if she even needed to breathe. It was all about dramatic effect with her. "But no matter. I'll get rid of all of you, then go back to work on him and the good doctor. Luna Lane's oldest human residents, besides this stubborn old fool." She hitched a thumb at Milton. "I'll just blame any deaths on this little wolfy thrall who'd do *anything* for me before I sucked him dry." Her eyebrows arched playfully.

Grady whimpered behind me.

"Why Falcon?" I demanded to know.

"The young taste so sweet," she said. "And that one was always wandering between the café and the bar as his parents got it ready to close. With the bustle of opening the pub at the same time, he made for a quick, easy snack many a night." She licked her lips. "He said it tickled. And because he was so hooked on the venom, he'd do anything I asked. Even go kidnap an old, musty man and bring him to me where no one might come across us as I sucked him dry once and for all. Wouldn't you, little one?" She cooed that last part, like talking to a puppy.

Falcon looked up at her, his tongue hanging down from his open mouth.

"Unfortunately, *some* addicts can't just wait their turns," she snapped into the darkness behind her. "Practically making me drag her around the pub, clutching at my leg before Mr. Perfect Mayor showed up to pull her away. Thankfully, my first progeny had stopped by, too—so serious, so *grumpy*. But little matter. He took care of them both for me."

Chione and Abdel. Draven had *taken care* of them?

My heart jumped into my throat. I felt so naïve for not realizing any of this earlier.

But the vampires had practically founded this town along with Abdel. I never would have expected it of them.

They didn't turn locals, like the vampires in the old country were wont to do. They didn't turn bloodbags into addicts. We all knew that. Abdel prided himself on that.

But they did. Hadn't I been the one to determine that?

"You made everyone in Milton's generation blood mad," I said, the theory passing across my lips in a whisper.

"No, I drank them all *dry*," she said, flipping her hair over her shoulders.

"Drank them dry?" I asked. "Then they died?" I hadn't known it was possible. I'd thought if vampires drank from someone too much, they simply turned.

"Passed away, moved away, drained of all blood from a vampire bite, what's the difference?" Ravana waved her hand, so callous, I wanted to scream at her. "I paid a price to the witch in the woods, and she helped me cover it all up. Made sure none of it seemed odd." She looked around at the desolate bowling alley. "Businesses shuttered, a generation moved on... No one questioned it. Pity. I did love the bowling alley. It was quite the fashion in the 1970s. But the owner was just another bloodbag on the list, and I'd gotten so bored of bowling with the same old group week in and week out. The list of bloodbags grew so small after a time. I couldn't kill *everyone* in town—even I had to draw the line somewhere. And then I had to slow down even more once the powerful enchantress moved out and the perky little do-gooder witch moved in."

Eithne. My mom would never have helped Ravana, that much was clear. "What price did you pay?" I asked from between gritted teeth.

Ravana looked amused. "To the witch? That's between her and me, sweetheart."

Let her keep her dark secret then. "The Davises weren't *drunk dry*."

"A few bloodbags went a little blood mad along the way. What can I say? It gets hard to keep track of how much venom each meal is receiving when you're sampling an entire town." Her incisor gleamed in the red glow of the flask in her hand. "If a blood mad bloodbag killed a couple of annoying other blood mad bloodbags along the way at my urging, I'd have been doing the town a favor." She examined the nails on one hand. "I'd gotten bored of Games Club by then anyway, all the fighting brought on by their addiction, Milton being so *rude* to me."

As if she didn't deserve that and more! "You made Leana kill the Davises!"

She shrugged. "I simply *encouraged* her to. Might have promised her more of my venom if she followed her husband and neighbors up into that attic that night they were all screaming and shut them all up. I hadn't even sat down to play yet, just watched them from the kitchen as they set the game up. The kitchen has an amazing view of the backyard. They kept arguing and arguing. It was so *dull*. The plan backfired, though. She couldn't kill Milton. And then her obstinate husband, too stupid to really realize that it was more than just blood madness, that *I'd urged* her to murder them all, tried to go back to normal for a bit. To pretend his wife hadn't smashed their best friends' heads in. Pretend he hadn't singlehandedly buried the bodies in the victims' own backyard to cover for her mistake." She snickered. "Eithne promised to make the Davises just *go away*, though because she's so *gleefully* devious, she refused to erase the Woodwards' memories of that evening.

So Milton thought one more Games Club might cheer his wife up. Make her forget it all happened. It didn't.

"I went because I wanted to see how my poor pet was faring, thinking maybe I could nudge her to finish the job. She was so distraught around me, he had to have realized the truth. But he wouldn't say the words, wouldn't accuse me of doing anything more than driving the rest of the club to addiction, not without admitting what he'd seen his wife do with his own two eyes. Poor Draven was so lost, but I managed to convince him Milton was just a jealous old bugger, angry the Davises and Leana had become bloodbags at all. As far as Draven knew, the Davises had moved, after all. Wasn't that proof I hadn't gone too far, hadn't made them truly addicted? Enough with the Woodwards. Games Club was *so* last decade." So Draven *hadn't* known about the murders? Something heavy settled in my stomach, something like guilt. Ravana continued. "Milton kept his wife away from me after that, long enough for her senses to return. I never had another chance to drink her dry. Not then anyway."

I gasped. "She didn't die of natural causes. You drank her dry in the attic!"

She smiled. "I did. I just had to wait for ol' Milton's mind to go so badly, his intent toward me changed, if just for a little while. I waited until Leana was upstairs, then I knocked on the door and he let me in. Thought it was time for Games Club.

Forgot how much he hated me." Her laughter was so obnoxious.

A muffled mumbling echoed out from somewhere in the dark behind her.

"What was that?" she asked sarcastically. "I'm afraid our mayor is a little *tied up* at the moment, but I'm sure he's saying something to the effect of, 'You'll never get away with this!' Oh, but I already have. For decades. Until the nosy, do-gooder witch junior stuck her nose where it wasn't welcomed."

"WOLG!" I said, more out of habit than anything. My hands didn't illuminate.

Ravana laughed, jiggling the red flask in her hand.

Out of the corner of my eye, I saw Cable had reached his uncle now and slipped a careful arm around him.

Ravana turned to them, and I knew I had to pull her focus back to me. "You said decades. How many? How many have you killed?"

Ravana licked her lips. "I've been drinking people dry for longer than you've been alive. 'Stick with the elderly,' I told myself. 'No one will think twice about an old person dropping dead.' But then they were gone, so I had to move on to the near-retirement. And the middle-aged."

That explained why Milton was the only really elderly person we had left in Luna Lane.

"But the elderly, even the middle-aged taste so... *stale*," she continued, tapping a red-manicured finger against the flask. "I've always much preferred children. But I've restrained myself."

"You're sick!" I shouted.

"Oh, stop. I'm a vampire. That's just what vampires do." She fluffed her hair. "You're lucky I didn't turn anyone in Luna Lane. No, *that* would be suspicious." Just as I'd thought. "So I had to leave to get my newest progeny in the old country." She glanced over her shoulder, probably at Mayor Abdel somewhere back there. It was the distraction I needed.

I jumped on Broomie's shaft and we flew toward Falcon, flying around widely to put as much distance between us and the red goo as we could. He looked up from his munching and growled.

"PEELS!" I shouted, pointing an arm at him.

But nothing happened. I was still too close to that flask. Curse me for ever even collecting it. I'd never even managed to run a successful test on it.

"Aren't you curious what this is?" Ravana asked, dangling the flask above her head.

"I have a feeling you'd love to tell me," I said simply, hovering above the now-leaping Falcon. He couldn't reach Broomie and me. Cable used the opportunity to carefully shuffle his uncle over to the next lane.

"I wasn't quite sure at first." She held it above her head and gazed at it, like it were a priceless jewel. "And if I'd have known it was up in the musty old man's rank attic, I would have gathered it ages ago, or at least when I was there to finish the job with Leana. Never know when a little para-para-normal might come in handy."

"Para-paranormal?" I asked. Falcon managed an especially high jump then and Broomie whimpered, just barely managing to fly us away.

"Oh, yes." A hand on her hip, Ravana walked down the lane, her heels alternatingly clopping and screeching against the surface her shoes weren't intended for. "I haven't seen it in... a millennia." Her eyes sparkled. "Because vampires and witches so rarely work together, at least not to an effect this great."

With a yelp, Falcon fell to the ground, landing on his back foot wrong and stumbling. Yowling, he ran off into the dark, leaving his father's mangled leg behind.

My heart thundered. The poor boy. Faine trusted me to look after him.

Broomie and I whirled on the approaching vampire, lowering. "You and Eithne planned this."

"Not at all. I highly doubt that skinflint enchantress would part with something so precious for nothing—my price paid did not *begin* to cover a stunning substance like this. But it looks like her enchantment on the game merged with my blood madness and together produced this." She stopped just a few feet away from me and shook the flask in the air.

And Broomie tumbled.

Screaming, I tried directing her up, pulling her upward, but she fell, clattering to the ground, my tailbone bruising as we hit the hard surface of the lane together.

"Ow, ow, ow," I cried out, rubbing my backside. My eyes widened and I picked up my pet, my trusted partner, my friend. "Broomie! Broomhilde!"

Ravana *tsked*. "I was wondering if and when it would affect her. It *should* affect every paranormal creature. It just seems to do so differently. Perhaps your broomstick needs very close exposure or..." She popped the cork. "Direct contact for safe measure."

"No!" I screamed, and as Ravana tilted the flask toward Broomie's brush, I threw my body over her, the hot, burning goo hitting my back instead.

Ravana laughed and the burning sensation stopped. I turned to look. Half of the red ectoplasm was still in the flask, though more was around her feet, the smallest bit on the toe of her red high-heeled shoe.

"Dark magic meets dark magic," Ravana explained. "And produces para-paranormal ecto-plasm as the result of a death. Or two. Or three. I knew when Draven purchased that enchanted, knockoff game from that enchantress, I would have so much *fun* with it. But *this*?"

"Draven *purchased* it?" He'd not only known Eithne all along, he'd brought the cursed game into this mess! The fiend!

"For a price." Her eyes sparkled. "Little did I know with that *toy*, I could have created this the whole time!" She grew mesmerized by the ectoplasm in her hand.

Cursing under my breath, I sat up. "You just wasted half of it."

"Oh, I can make more if I find the right witch —and *you're* the one who alerted the town to Eithne's return." She whipped her head around. Cable and Milton were back by the chairs, shuffling on quiet feet past Grady. "But first I plan on feeding on that brat who'd never offer us vampires even a taste." Her nose wrinkled. "He must taste so, so *musty* by now, but I don't care. He deserves to be drunk dry just like his wife finally was!" She scoffed. "He took Leana from me! She refused me for *years*! For *decades*! But I wouldn't stand for it. I wouldn't let it go."

Cable tugged on his uncle, but Milton tugged back, shaking his head. They argued in harsh tones and Milton broke free, shuffling at an unexpected speed toward the ball return.

"The game didn't lead to the murders at all?" I asked, half by way of distraction, half because I needed to know the truth. What had Draven expected from Eithne when he'd bought a cursed game and brought it to Games Club?

Ravana sneered. "That Evidence game is just a harmless bit of dark magic. Nothing too out of the ordinary in Luna Lane, well, especially before a certain do-gooder witch and her do-gooder little brat turned up to make the place so *bright* and *cheery* all the time." She stuck her tongue out.

"But if you win," I ventured, grasping at any way to explain it, hoping she'd take the bait and correct me if I was wrong, "the character cards change—"

"No, if you *lose*. Am I the only one who figured that out?" She rolled her eyes. "If you're the murderer and you get called out by another player before you leave the game. Then your card changes to someone in town. Heaven if I know why it chooses which person to change into."

"It was the person they most admired," I said.

"Charming." Her voice was droll. I'd bet my last dollar that Ravana wouldn't know anything about admiring *anyone*.

There were noises behind Ravana of a struggle, and she turned to see, but I pulled her back to me, rubbing the sore spot on my back.

"So what was the point? Why did Draven buy a cursed game from a wicked witch?"

She shrugged. "It was a harmless bit of fun, as he saw it. Make the illustrations move. Have the game change and mold itself to the players. Why play just a normal board game in a spooky, para-normal town?"

Why indeed? But Draven couldn't be that inno-cent. It didn't make sense. He'd *bought* it from Eithne! From an evil witch! He'd paid some kind of price when he'd told me himself most people weren't willing to pay what the witch would ask for.

"But I don't think he ever expected the game to… Well, I don't think he ever figured out what Leana managed to," Ravana continued. "*I* didn't know until that night a few months ago when I followed her into her attic."

"Figured out what?"

Ravana smiled widely. "Wouldn't you like to know? You're so good at sticking your nose into other people's business, why don't you figure it out for yourself? Say, did you ever finish playing a round of the game?"

"No…" I mentally kicked myself for not following Roan's suggestion. But it would have been impossible with Draven and Abdel gone anyway.

It hit me then. Virginia's account of how *noisy* it had been in the game. The game being there during the murder of the Davises. Being nearby when Leana had been sucked dry. The "para-paranormal" ectoplasm that resulted from death and the crossing of two kinds of paranormal energies.

"They're there," I said softly. "Jessmyn, Abraham, and even Leana… They're trapped in the game!" Just like Virginia had been. But her, getting there through different means… Perhaps they hadn't been able to communicate that to her.

Ravana laughed. "So you're smart enough to figure things out after all. That was what Leana told me, anyway, as she'd begged not for salvation, but for just a few more minutes of life to *free* her friends' souls. I couldn't have cared less." She tapped her foot, the shoe with the glob of red para-paranormal. "But then when she drew her last breath, I saw it for myself. That game, in her hands, shuddered and flew open, then it ripped Leana's soul clean out of her body and inside it. I stuffed it as far up out of the way as I could manage and decided to let them rot there." Her eyes gleamed. "Souls that die from blood madness aren't always destined for a happier place. I suppose, in some small measure, being trapped in the game gives them time to collect themselves and move on to that *better* place. Unless, of course, they never move on at all." She laughed and laughed. And beneath that laughter was a *clunk* and then the rolling of a ball.

With a shriek, Ravana only seemed to notice when the bowling ball came into contact with her ankle.

Chapter Twenty-Two

"*S*trike!" Milton's shout carried down the lane, and he danced a jig in place as Cable watched, slack-jawed.

Ravana fumbled for her leg, gritting her teeth, but her shoe slipped, and I launched forward to rip it off her foot. Then I flipped it around and stuck the glob of para-paranormal right against her flesh.

She screamed like the Wicked Witch of the West doused in water.

"You *witch!*" She swung at me, hissing, her incisors like a predator's on full display. I grabbed her calf and pulled as hard as I could, yanking her to the ground. Her cheek hit the hard lane with a crack, her flesh straight in the para-paranormal she'd spilled off my back so carelessly.

She started steaming, the hiss escaping her lips only drowned out by the searing of her skin, the clatter of the flask to the ground. Its cork still off, it started spilling out.

I scrambled on top of her prone form and we both struggled for the flask. She scratched at me and then turned and bit my arm—I screamed, but only one fang poked flesh, just lightly. The other bounced against a stone scale with a sickening *crunch*. She pulled back and cradled her jaw, as if she'd cracked a tooth.

The flask was in my hands again, but no matter, it was everywhere, spread out across the lane. I kicked the flask and the last of the goo down the back end of the lane and snatched Broomie out of the way. A bit of the goo got on her bristles and I whapped them desperately. She was so stiff in my hands. Like a normal broom.

Ravana rose up on shaky forearms, her beautiful face bubbling with the red substance. "Aw'll get thoo!" she said, and I realized one of her incisors had snapped in half, no longer a pointy threat. "You witch! You will pay!"

An echo of snarling broke out into the bowling alley as Faine and her girls leaped through the broken window and bolted down the lane. Faine's attention caught on Grady's prone body immediately and she yowled, pulling up beside him. She nudged him and he tapped her softly with his tail.

Cable jumped up on top of one of the chairs, as if that would save him from a hungry wolf, and with a strength that seemed almost inhuman, he yanked his uncle up to follow him.

The girls were too focused on their father to care, though. They shivered up against each other.

Faine whirled on Ravana and growled, her ears flat against her head. She took a step forward and then stopped, glancing at her paw.

The very tip of it was turning back into a human hand.

How?

The para-paranormal.

She couldn't get any closer to it, not without losing her advantage.

A little yipping echoed out from the darkness and Falcon trotted over to his mom, his head hung low. On his back was Chione and Abdel, both wrapped up together in Abdel's own wrappings, pulled loose. Chione had passed out, the bags still dark under her eyes. Abdel's skin looked ashen, his handsome face fading fast without the tight, controlled magic of his mummy wrappings.

In the presence of this para-paranormal goo all around my feet.

Ravana dragged herself up to her knees.

"Fray-fen!" she snapped. "Fray-fen, get out f-here!"

All was silent but for Faine's growling for a few moments and then with a *clomp*, *clomp*, *clomp* against the hard floor of the lanes, Draven appeared from out in the darkness, from where

Falcon had emerged with Chione and Abdel in tow.

"Frink them!" Ravana stood up shakily and pointed at me, at Faine, at everyone. "Frink them fry!"

Draven cupped an ear. "Sorry, I didn't catch that!"

Ravana's eyes widened. "Frink them! Frink their flood!"

Draven crossed his arms and looked down. "If I can't understand you, you can't blame me for not obeying your orders."

A guttural noise escaped Ravana's lips, like a wounded animal cornered but not willing to give up. "Uth-less! Uth-less fampire!"

Her eyes rolled to the back of her head and she laughed, the sound choked. With the last of her strength, she leaped.

Straight for me.

I whirled, tossing Broomie as far away as I could. Faine jumped up and caught her just as Ravana latched on to me, her remaining incisor grazing across my neck.

I closed my eyes. This was it for me.

But that was okay. If it gave everyone else time to get away from her…

Ravana's incisor hit something hard again with a *crack*.

I blinked. She hadn't pierced my flesh.

"Lia? Faine? Grady?" Roan and Qarinah stumbled onto the scene over by the chairs, too far away to have been the ones to stop Ravana.

Ravana shrieked and fell back, and I felt something strange slide across my neck, though I couldn't see anything at all.

It was like… Lace. Lace and a hard tip.

There was an indistinct pale white glow.

Blinking, I willed my eyes to find a way to see her.

Virginia, almost translucent, floated in front of me, her folded lace parasol resting over one shoulder against her neck in an echo of what she must have done for me. Ravana had bit down hard on Virginia's porcelain parasol ferrule made corporeal, cracking her last venom-filled tooth.

"About time you noticed I was here." Virginia smiled broadly.

I stumbled toward her and embraced her, my fingers falling through air until she grew brighter and brighter and managed to take form to hug me back.

Chapter Twenty-Three

I sat on the swing seat on Faine's front porch, wearing the borrowed vintage blue polka dot dress she'd given me, petting Broomie absentmindedly. Goldie sat beside me, just holding my hand. Broomie cooed as she stretched out across both our laps.

My hair was damp against my bare shoulders. I'd taken a shower—a real one—to clear the para-paranormal away. My dress was ruined, but my hat, that was important. Faine promised to clean it and give it back to me, along with my belt. But that was far from the most important issue right now.

The door to the house opened with a squeak.

"How are they?" I asked Faine as she stepped out.

She stared at the horizon, at the black sky becoming blue as the dawn began approaching.

"Much better," she said, smiling at me, as if

remembering I was there for the first time. She looked exhausted but relieved. "Thanks to you."

The para-paranormal washed away, I'd been able to heal Grady's arm—mostly. It had worked and he was okay, but the arm was horribly scarred, healed bite wounds mangling the flesh. I didn't know why I couldn't fix that, but Grady had put a hand on my stony arm and told me it was okay.

Falcon hadn't needed anything more than a sleep enchantment, which I'd given to his wound-up sisters as well, with their parents' blessing. Falcon would have to be watched closely for at least a few weeks so he could work through his addiction to vampire venom, even if Ravana was in custody in the vampires' basement and I trusted Qarinah and Draven to leave him alone. Roan's lone jail cell needed fixing, and besides, Ravana needed to be in a coffin at daybreak or she'd die for good.

I shouldn't have cared if she did, but I didn't want her to have the pleasure of knowing we weren't any better than her before she passed.

Draven had written to Transylvania, sent the letter express somehow only vampires knew how to. Someone would come for her in the night, and she'd be out of Luna Lane forever. Vampires in the old country didn't have many rules, but they frowned on driving bloodbags blood mad or drinking them dry rather than turning them.

So it was over now. Roan had promised to come up with a story for the county—maybe even produce a death certificate for Milton, forged by town hall and Doc Day. Whatever it would take to get them off our backs.

The kids and Grady slept peacefully upstairs. The whole family had actually turned human earlier than they normally would have on the night of the full moon, the red ectoplasm having some slow, muted effect on their own abilities, especially as I'd hobbled over covered in the goo. Time would tell if they would even change next full moon. We were in new territory, though that was, thankfully, the last of the stuff.

"Lia," Roan called up from the sidewalk. He'd stayed behind with Cable to clean up all the para-paranormal, Abdel and Chione stepping out for fresh air and to readjust Abdel's wrappings. Abdel had saved his granddaughter from her addiction by temporarily wrapping her up in some of his enchanted wrappings, but the process had made them both too weak to resist Draven capturing them at the pub and taking them to the bowling alley on Ravana's command. With Abdel's wrappings read-justed, he was back to his normal self, and Chione seemed over her blood addiction fast. But he'd insisted the magic wouldn't work on anyone but his family, so there was no hope of a speedy recovery for Falcon.

Qarinah and Draven had taken Milton—at his request—next door to their home.

He'd wanted to see Ravana imprisoned. He'd

been clear enough to ask that.

"Sheriff," I said, nodding.

"We have to finish the game." He gestured a thumb over his shoulder at the vampires' house next door. "Let's hurry. Qarinah and Draven need to get to bed."

I jolted upright. How could I have forgotten?

"Go," said Faine, clasping her hands together. "We'll watch her." She nodded at the purring, sleeping Broomie and Goldie smiled.

"You have some fun now, dear," Goldie added.

I didn't have time to explain how we weren't about to have fun at all.

Running down the steps, I cut across the yard and headed next door, meeting up with Roan as we approached the front step.

Inside, Cable, Chione, Abdel, and Virginia lingered in the dining room. Abdel had a hand on Chione's shoulder, and she nodded solemnly, her eyes on the ground and her arms crossed. She perked up hopefully when Qarinah appeared at the top of the basement stairs, but the vampire just shook her head at Chione and took her hand. The mayor's granddaughter may have been clean of the vampire venom, but it was clear a part of her still craved it.

"No more, dear," she said. "I couldn't drink from you again—not after what Ravana did to you."

Chione's face fell and Abdel consoled her. "You

are no bloodbag. You were meant for greater things, child."

Draven stepped up from the basement, shutting the door behind him with a *clank*. He looked at me, and his eyes darted downward. "Let's hurry," he said. "I finished sealing Ravana's coffin shut, but Qarinah and I need to get down there, too."

He strode into the dining room and sat down at the table without another word.

"Miss Poplar!" said Virginia, floating up beside me. Cable watched, amused, and then left to join his uncle, who sat at a chair at the dining room table. Virginia spoke excitedly. "Cable was telling me— you think Leana's and the others' souls are trapped in the game?"

I nodded. "We need to finish and find out."

Virginia frowned. "I do wish I'd have figured that out while I'd been in there."

I put a hand on her arm—solid, cold, but real. "You did more than enough," I pointed out. "Thank you, friend."

She beamed and floated to find a spot beside Chione next to Milton and Cable.

The board game was a little messed up from Virginia climbing right out of it, but nothing was irrevocably out of place. I quickly shifted things back as they were and sat down in front of my game sheet. "Whose turn was it?" I asked.

Draven picked up the dice without a word and handed them to Abdel, who took his turn.

It was awful solemn for a few rounds, the only sound Virginia's humming and Milton's soft, croaking voice calling out his wife's name.

"Draven," I said quietly to the vampire beside me as Qarinah and Roan took their joint turn. "Did you know? About Ravana drinking too much from Luna Lane's citizens?"

He grew stiff. "I suspected. She forbade any discussion of it. Now that I know she relied on Eithne's magic for a time, it all seems clearer. But there was always a perfect excuse to explain an absence in town. The enchantment made it so none of us would examine such things too deeply."

"So *you* never drank anyone dry or to the point of blood madness."

"Of course not." His eyes narrowed on me.

He seemed to find evidence on my face of what I'd thought for a while—that he and Ravana had been in on the blood madness, the murders, together. There was still something I needed to know.

"Hmm," said Abdel loudly, stroking his cloth-covered chin.

It was my turn. I uncovered one more clue and realized... Realized I knew the who, the how, and the where.

I could win this game.

I opened my mouth and Draven gripped my hand, squeezing it.

He shook his head at me and nodded toward the

board.

Qarinah and Roan's character, Dreadful Darling, was just a few spaces away from sneaking out the back door.

Dreadful was the killer this round. I'd just discovered it had been with the meat cleaver in the bedroom.

But something Milton kept saying. Play the game again. Finish the game. Winning *the right way*.

If I won this way, Qarinah and Roan would get caught. They'd lose, and next time, a character card might change to depict whomever Qarinah or Roan admired most. But that wasn't our aim at all.

"You were right," said Milton softly. "We just have to win the right way."

I clamped my mouth shut.

Draven took his turn and uncovered a clue in the billiards room with a bored expression on his face.

"You bought this game from Eithne," I said simply. "You kept that from me." The rest may have been out of his hands, beyond his knowledge, but that... That was worse than keeping the fact that Eithne had once lived in Luna Lane from me.

"*'I'll turn them into a frog and keep them in a one-foot-wide aquarium for the rest of their days,'*" he parroted back at me. "Do you think I could admit to you that I commissioned the game from your sworn enemy after you said that?"

My palms grew sweaty, and I realized the game

had stopped, that everyone was watching us.

"It was just a bit of fun," Draven said. "I truly thought it might make Games Club more exciting. If I'd known about what Ravana was doing, I would have never risked the magics mixing. But I wanted to believe in her. She's my sire. I knew she looked down on other creatures, but I never thought... She seemed to have *fun* playing games and bowling. At first anyway. I thought she was starting to care a little. Oh, Dahlia. I'm so sorry."

He looked contrite. Truly. I'd never seen him so genuine. But my heart was thundering and I wasn't sure I could forgive him, even though I knew he was right. I'd made it impossible for him to confess. Still, I wasn't about to admit that. Did he think I'd *actually* turn him into a frog? "*Sorry?* You think just saying *sorry* is enough—"

"Stop!" Milton shouted. "If you can't get along, then what's the point of Games Club?"

We all stared at him. I'd raised my voice, but no one had been arguing. Not really.

"I *told* you giving those vampires blood was a bad idea! Look at you! Look at the lot of you, about to rip each other's throats out! Don't you laugh, *harlot*! You do nothing but take, take, take from this town! Well, get out! All of you! I'll stash this away rather than let you keep fighting like this!"

Cable calmed his uncle down and Virginia said, "Oh. That must be what he was saying when he ran upstairs with the game in hand all those years ago."

268

On the night Leana had gone truly blood mad and murdered their best friends, her vampire puppet master putting thoughts in her head.

We were all quiet for a bit, but Qarinah jumped, probably realizing she and Draven were running short on time.

She rolled, and letting out a small giggle, moved her and Roan's character piece right out the backyard.

"Ha!" she cried. "We did it! With the meat cleaver in the bedroom and we got away!"

Roan chuckled as Qarinah hugged him and then…

The board started shaking.

The three character cards that had changed soared toward the board.

They moved in circles above it, a visible surge of energy passing between the board and the cards.

And then, like Virginia had crawled out of the board, so did Leana.

Pale, younger than I remembered her, and semi-translucent.

Behind her crawled the Abraham I'd seen in pictures, and then Jessmyn, the three spirits floating high above the board game.

The cards clattered down and the board went quiet. I noticed the illustrations on the cards had changed to people unfamiliar to me.

"Leana." Milton stood and reached up toward her.

"Milton," she said softly. "I'm sorry… I'm sorry I ever put you through this."

"No," he said. "No, it wasn't you."

Her eyes watered. "I wanted to save them."

"You were the one who figured out they were stuck in the game, that there was more to the magic in the game. You wanted to play again—and I got angry." He started crying, more lucid than he'd been in ages. "I'm sorry. You were right, though. We just didn't win the right way when we played. The killer wasn't one of us—the killer didn't get away."

"I got the game down again," said Leana softly. "I was going to bring it downstairs. But when I turned around—"

"She was there," said Milton. "The blood-sucking harlot." His eyes went glassy, his words devolving to mumbling.

Leana smiled sadly and turned to the other spirits. "I know she made me blood mad, but I can never, ever forgive myself."

"We forgive you. We told you." Jessmyn smiled and took Abraham's hand. His lips upturned into a broad grin, too.

"We do. Leana, we know what blood madness can do. We're grateful you stopped us from hurting anyone ourselves."

Leana shook her head. An afterimage followed the slow movement.

"I wished I'd never let her drink me."

"Us, too," said Jessmyn. "But that's over now.

And we know you figured it out—that you intended to set us free that night you joined us."

Still holding hands, the couple held arms out to Leana. "It's time to go," said Abraham. "The time in the game… We've cleansed our souls. Let's go. To the other side. To a better place."

"Leana." Milton reached up, but his hand passed through her feet.

Leana turned around and smiled, but she was already floating away. She took hold of Abraham's and Jessmyn's hands, the three forming a circle.

"Thank you," they said as one.

They closed their eyes, and with a great gust of wind, they flew up and were gone.

"They passed," said Virginia after a moment of silence.

"Draven." I turned to my ex-boyfriend. I needed to apologize. Even if I wasn't still entirely over it.

But he was gone. Qarinah, too.

"They had to get in their coffins," explained Roan.

I hadn't even noticed them leave. Now I'd have to wait to speak to Draven. Maybe the right time would never come.

"Well," said Abdel, standing and straightening his suit jacket. "That was a memorable game night."

Everyone left in the room looked at one another and laughed.

Chapter Twenty-Four

"So…" I said to Cable as he, Milton, and I stopped in front of his house. Milton shuffled up the walkway and inside the house without comment, and we were both quiet as we watched through the window to make sure he made it inside safely. He sat in his chair in front of his TV and promptly, it seemed, fell asleep.

Broomie still purred in her slumber, curled up in my arms.

"She's like a cat," said Cable, holding a finger above her brush hesitatingly.

I laughed. "She has a cat's soul."

"Huh?" He stopped just short of petting her.

"You can pet her," I said. He did, and a smile lit up his face as she instinctively arched up into his touch. "She's not so scary after all, is she?"

He chuckled. "No, I guess not… But a cat's soul?"

"After a cat's ninth life, it can move on to the place beyond or stick around in another form. The ones with a particular talent for magic usually attach themselves to witches' brooms." I nodded at her. "Broomie's been with me since birth."

"Nine lives, huh? I thought at least *some things* were still just myths."

I patted Broomie's brush. "I'm sure there are plenty of myths still out there. You're not going to investigate them and make your big break in the journalism world?"

"No, thank you." He beamed. "I never even wanted to be a journalist. I just said that to rattle you."

"You're certainly braver than the little Cable I remember visiting town."

"I'm glad you're starting to remember." He clamped his lips together tightly, but his dark eyes sparkled with amusement.

"Does that mean you're not going to pack up and leave early?" I asked.

"Are you kidding me? No way." He scratched the back of his head, and I was drawn to the way the dark shadow growing across his cheeks made him look even more handsome. "When Mom suggested spending my sabbatical in Luna Lane, I jumped at the chance to confirm whether or not everything she'd told me, all my repressed memories, were true. And then I get here, and everyone's trying so hard to keep the paranormal out of my sight! Quite a disappointment."

"Well, not *everyone*. Pretty much just me."

"Yeah, mostly just you." He chuckled. "But wow, I was still in for quite a few surprises. Is it always this hectic in Luna Lane?"

"Not at all," I said. "Quite quiet, usually. It's almost like you showed up and jinxed us all."

"Maybe I'm paranormal, too." He snorted. "Is there anything like a bad luck monster around?"

"Not since the harpy mermaid moved out of town." I smirked. I was only joking.

He laughed too. He didn't seem sure whether or not I was joking.

I avoided eye contact, enjoying being the one to tease him.

"Well," said Cable as he took a step back. "See you around?"

"Sure," I said, ready to sleep the rest of the day.

"Maybe at Games Club?"

I chuckled. Then I stopped. He was teasing me, right?

I whirled around, but he'd already stepped inside Milton's house.

My hand clutched the handle to my front door. A bit of ivy from my overgrown yard had snaked through the porch overhang and hung in front of my face.

Broomie sat up in my arms and stretched, flying around me in a circle.

"No time to fly," I told her. "I need a long, long nap."

Broomie poked my side.

I tried to wave her away, but that piece of ivy brushed across my nose.

A flower bloomed in front of my face.

"Don't forget," said a disembodied voice with a slight accent. My spine stiffened. Eithne. I spun around, but she was nowhere to be found, the voice carrying on purple dust emanating from the white flower on the vine. *"One good deed per day,"* it said.

Bananaberries. I couldn't risk falling asleep and missing the entire day again.

Scratching my arm and the newest scale, I turned on my heel.

Across the way, Arjun was unlocking the front door to Vogel's, but he was struggling because he was balancing several boxes and a tote bag stuffed with produce Jeremiah must have dropped off at his home earlier this morning.

Taking a deep breath and gesturing at myself, I said, "YGRENE," banishing my exhaustion better than I could even with Faine's tasty coffee.

I jumped up on Broomie and we soared across the yard to the general store.

"Arjun!" I cried. "Let me help you with that."

Join the Spooky Games Club in
Enchantments and Escape Rooms!

After the disaster of the month before, Dahlia Poplar, cursed witch and helper extraordinaire, is ready for her serene, supernatural small town life to return to normal. However, her hopes for a more peaceful existence don't last when a childhood friend moves back to Luna Lane to open up an escape room.

With the Spooky Games Club thriving, Dahlia decides to help her friend by using her magic to quickly get his business up and running. Dahlia's enchantments accomplish the task, but before the Games Club has a chance to enjoy the new attraction, a test of the escape room results in a freak, fatal accident. Riddled with guilt, Dahlia wonders where her enchantments went wrong—or if there's something more to the disaster.

The only way to divine whether or not the death was her fault, the result of an accident, or murder is to investigate—and perhaps even play the dangerous game herself. In this one-hour escape room, failure to escape could mean death, not just for Dahlia, but for those she holds most dear.

About the Author

Amy McNulty is an editor and author of books that run the gamut from YA speculative fiction to contemporary romance. A lifelong fiction fanatic, she fangirls over books, anime, manga, comics, movies, games, and TV shows from her home state of Wisconsin. When not reviewing anime professionally or editing her clients' novels, she's busy fulfilling her dream by crafting fantastical worlds of her own.

Sign up for Amy's newsletter to receive news and exclusive information about her current and upcoming projects. Get a free YA romantic sci-fi novelette when you do!

Find her at amymcnulty.com and follow her on social media:

amazon.com/author/amymcnulty

bookbub.com/authors/amy-mcnulty

facebook.com/AmyMcNultyAuthor

twitter.com/mcnultyamy

instagram.com/mcnulty.amy

pinterest.com/authoramymc

Look for More Speculative Fiction
Reads from Crimson Fox Publishing

Crimson Fox
PUBLISHING

Alexandra's Riddle

ELISA KEYSTON

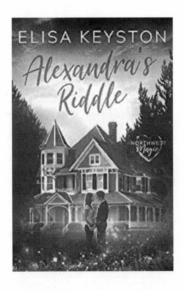

Lose yourself in the magical forests and charming towns of the Pacific Northwest, where picturesque Victorian homes hide mysteries spanning decades, faeries watch

from the trees, and romance awaits... for those bold enough to seek it.

Cass is a drifter. When she inherits an old Queen Anne Victorian in rural Oregon from her great-aunt Alexandra, all she wants is to quickly offload the house and move on to bigger and better things. But the residents of the small town have other plans in mind. Her neighbors are anxious for her to help them thwart the plans of a land developer eager to raze Alexandra's property, while a mysterious girl in the woods needs Cass's help understanding her own confusing, possibly supernatural abilities.

And though little surprises Cass (thanks to her own magical powers of prediction), she never could have anticipated her newfound feelings for the handsome fourth-grade teacher at the local elementary school —feelings that she thought she'd buried long ago. Cass has sworn off love, but Matthew McCarthy is unlike anyone Cass has ever met. If she isn't careful, he could learn her secret. Or worse—he just might thaw her frozen heart.

But falling in love could spell danger for both of them. Because it's not just the human residents of Riddle that have snared Cass in their web. Cass's presence has caught the attention of the fae that dwell in the woods. They know she has the Sight, and they don't want to let her go...

With its unique blend of small-town romance, cozy mystery, and light fantasy, the Northwest Magic series is sure to delight anyone who believes in faery gifts and happily-ever-afters. Read FREE in Kindle Unlimited and get lost in the magic now!

Destruction

SHARON BAYLISS

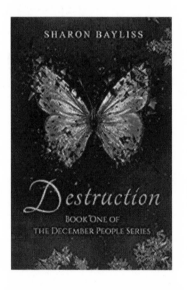

David Vandergraff wants to be a good man. He goes to church every Sunday, keeps his lawn trim and green, and loves his wife and kids more than anything. Unfortunately, being a dark wizard isn't a choice.

Eleven years ago, David's secret second family went missing. When his two lost children are finally found, he learns they suffered years of unthinkable abuse. Ready to make things right, David brings the kids home even though it could mean losing the wife he can't imagine living without.

Keeping his life together becomes harder when the new children claim to be dark wizards. David believes they use this fantasy to cope with their trauma. Until, David's wife admits a secret of her own—she is a dark wizard too, as is David, and all of their children.

Now, David must parent two hurting children from a dark world he doesn't understand and keep his family from falling apart. All while dealing with the realization that everyone he loves, including himself, may be evil.